UTE PEAK COUNTRY

Jackson Miggs is a trapper who winters under Ute Peak in his log cabin. A loner, he doesn't care much for small spaces or crowds, but is amiable enough with cowman Hyatt Tolman, who grazes his herd in the nearby high meadows. Tolman's friend Frank McCoy takes Miggs's pelts out in the fall, sells them at Fort Laramie and Cheyenne, then brings him the proceeds in the spring. But this year, McCoy arrives accompanied by the beautiful Beverly Shafter and a herd of Durham cattle — which he moves right onto the grazing land that the Tolman herd has used for years. As tensions mount, trouble is coming to Ute Peak country . . .

SPECIAL MESSAGE TO READERS

First published in the United States by Center Point

First Isis Edition
published 2018
by arrangement with
Golden West Literary Agency

A catalogue record for this book is available
from the British Library.

ISBN 978–1–78541–398–8 (pb)

Published by
F. A. Thorpe (Publishing)
Anstey, Leicestershire

Set by Words & Graphics Ltd.
Anstey, Leicestershire
Printed and bound in Great Britain by
T. J. International Ltd., Padstow, Cornwall

UTE PEAK COUNTRY

LAURAN PAINE

SAGEBRUSH
Large Print Westerns

CHAPTER
ONE

There was a brisk, cold wind blowing down the cañons. Where it came funneling to the gray grasslands under that overhead, leaden sky, it whipped around and beat back upon the foothills punishing them with its cutting chill.

Clouds scudded from north to south, gray-edged, ragged, and rushing headlong down the alien sky. Spring was close but winter had not yet surrendered; it sent its marshaled forces in reckless and headlong charge to the far curving of prairie, there to hurl its frigid blasts against that warmer air coming northward.

Ute Peak stood bulky and immense, its sides corrugated from the eternal struggles that took place in the high country between spring and winter each year, its rough-cut peak where the everlasting snow field lay, alternately dead-white and pink, alternately reflecting the mood of those soiled clouds, or the thin shafts of sunlight that occasionally broke through to strike up there.

Otherwise the land was rough, rocky, tilted-to-flowing, wild, uninhabited mostly, scourged by elements and shunned by most men, except in the spring when lowland cowmen drove herds to the parks,

1

the meadows, and the great grassland plateaus where an indigenous tough, wiry short grass grew that put more grease under a critter's hide in thirty days than he'd otherwise get in five months of hay feeding.

Except for this, perhaps, the lowland people would have only come to the Ute Peak country to hunt elk, deer, and bear.

Up here were blue-blurred ranks of spruce growing upon granite escarpments where a pine couldn't grow. But lower, near the meadows, ringing them around, were the firs, the pines, even some raffish old junipers. Here one had no trouble encountering bears and lions, and, like now with spring close by, rutting bull elks large as a horse with swollen necks and bloodshot eyes, more to be feared in this, their mating season, than a she-bear with cubs.

The cattlemen didn't normally make their upland drives until the last snowfall was surely past, but this was not always so, for the first cattle into the high country had that much head start on a weight gain over subsequent herds, so usually some bold spirit brought his critters up the torturous trail out of the lowland, settled parts of Colorado, in late April, or sometimes in mid-May.

But one thing was certain. With that gusty bitter wind pushing those gray-lined clouds, the game would return and with it would come men, for this was the heavenward sign of burgeoning springtime, and a man like Jackson Miggs, who had wintered under Ute Peak in his strong log cabin with its six-foot ceiling and its two-foot solid log walls, was ready to welcome anyone,

2

even the cowmen whose animals spoiled his trout streams and closely cropped the forage, driving elk and deer higher up into the saw-toothed back-country mountains.

Jackson Miggs was no more than five feet seven inches tall but Mother Nature had rammed a lot of sheer brute strength down into that tough hide of his. Jack weighed two hundred pounds and could match the death hug of a two-year-old bear, muscle for muscle. Legend said that he'd actually done it, had actually stood up one time when a young shag back had reared up at him from behind a tree, and had before three cowboys from Hyatt Tolman's outfit met that bear face to face and had locked his immense arms around the bear, squeezed harder than the shag back could hug, left the bear unconscious in a thin snowbank, and laughed.

Those thoroughly awed range riders had taken that story back down to the Pagosa plains when they'd returned to the settlement country with the last drags of Tolman's cattle. It had been good for many a free drink in the Pagosa saloons, too, as all such stories were.

But Jackson Miggs never profited from it. He only went to Pagosa once or twice a year. Even then he wouldn't go if he could inveigle someone else into fetching back supplies for him. Jackson Miggs didn't like civilization. He liked people, but not mobs of them. He once told Frank McCoy that towns made him feel panicky, that when he looked out a window and saw a building across the road less than two hundred feet away, he felt like things were closing in on him.

He told Frank McCoy a lot of things, and Frank, in return for Jack's friendship in that lonely world up under Ute Peak, packed Miggs's winter-trapped pelts and plews out for Jack every fall, sold them at Fort Laramie or farther east, in Cheyenne, hid the money, dug it up again in the spring, and brought it back to Miggs on his way into the Ute Peak country from the north. In fact, it was usually with this north wind at his back that Frank came angling down out of some dark and twisted cañon, bundled to the eyes in a blanket coat, with a shawl over his head and ears, tied under his throat, and his broad-brimmed black Stetson hat snugged down tightly over the shawl.

That was why, when the gusts would momentarily diminish, Miggs would look up from where he was chopping at the woodpile, and run a searching look out and around. The storms had been scudding past for ten days now, too high, too fast moving under the bitter wind, to dump more snow downward, but bound instead for the lowland country where they would dump rain. To a knowledgeable man like Jackson Miggs, or to one like Frank McCoy, this was the sign of spring.

But McCoy didn't come that day, or the next day, either. He didn't come swinging down out of a northward cañon for another seven days, and then he did not come alone, nor did he announce his arrival as he usually did with a ringing loud Ute scream. But even so, riding steadily through lingering night shadows out

4

of a cañon's mouth, Jack Miggs caught his movement thirty seconds before even an Indian would have.

Jack was sitting outside on a bench with his back to the rough front wall of his house doing nothing, just sitting there letting the thin sunbeams beat against him, thawing his winter-hardened marrow. Even after he saw McCoy, he didn't move. In fact, not until Frank reined back to let his companion come up beside him where the cañon ended and the meadow began, did Miggs even flicker an eye.

But then he did, because even at that distance it was obvious — swaddling coat, big hat tugged low, bear-skin gauntlets and all — that Frank's companion was a female.

Jack watched, sitting still like an Indian, until consternation stirred, then he got up, passed swiftly from sight inside his cabin, scooped up discarded clothes here and there, stuffed them into a closet, hid an earthenware jug of rye whiskey behind the stove, kicked at scattered whittlings near the woodbox, and darted to his mirror to comb hair and great shaggy beard. By then his dismay had crystallized into indignation, and if there was one thing Jackson Miggs could not do, it was keep how he felt from showing in his face, in his dead-level blue eyes and down around his wide, bearded mouth.

"He's in there!"

Jack put down the steel comb, squinted self-consciously at the mirror, and began to turn away.

"Hey you old south end of a bear, come out here!"

Miggs hastily pushed his woolen shirt into his trousers at the waistband, walked over, took a breath, and opened the door.

McCoy let off a bellow and stiffly climbed out of the saddle, his face, what of it was visible, corrugated with pleasure, his little pale eyes dancing.

"She's got a little mite of gray in 'er this year, that bush of yours, Jack, but I brought back a new straight razor so you can shed the underbrush."

Miggs stood uncertainly, near to smiling, his smoky glance jumping from McCoy on the ground to the girl still sitting atop her horse, and back again. He finally smiled, took two long steps forward, and roughly caught McCoy's ungloved and outstretched hand. They bawled at one another, wrenched each other's arms with powerful tugs, and beat each other upon the back.

"Come inside," said Miggs, "you dog-goned settlement man. You're late this spring but you're still the first to reach the uplands."

Frank McCoy turned, called to the girl to get down, to come along inside, then turned without another glance backward and went rolling along with his wide-shouldered, narrow-hipped gait, beside the short but vastly broader bulk of Jackson Miggs, into that massive log house with its little patches of dirty snow at the earth line and its stringy spiral of wood-stove smoke rising from the mud-wattle chimney overhead.

"Hey," roared McCoy, shedding his blanket coat, his head shawl, and hat, swinging his long arms, and standing back to the stove, "where's the jug of corn squeezings?"

6

"Where's my money?" countered Miggs, heading for the stove, halting though before he brought the jug forth because the girl had just entered, closed the door at her back, and stood there looking frail, looking small and out of place, but also smiling at the bear-like antics of those two rough men.

McCoy reached under his shirt, tugged out a fat money belt, and flung it upon the table. "Twenty-seven hundred dollars," he boomed. "Jack, you know what's going to happen to you someday? You're going to die up in here some wintertime and no one's ever going to know where you hide this damned money."

Miggs stood there, grinning but silent. He was watching the girl, and because he had been raised thinking womenfolk should never see menfolk drink hard liquor, he kept his back to the stove and the jug behind it, until McCoy turned, gazed over at him, and said: "Well, what you waitin' for you dog-goned old hidebound hermit? Fetch the jug out."

The girl removed her hat, her head shawl, those hair-side-out, bear-skin gauntlets, and her coat. With all those things discarded she was no more than a slip of a female. Jack thought that, wringing wet, she wouldn't have weighed more than a hundred and five or ten pounds — and that, with both pockets full of stones.

But it was well distributed, that hundred and five or ten pounds. She was as pretty as a picture with her jet-black wavy hair, her steel gray eyes like forming smoke from a winter campfire, and her red lips that gently lifted at their outer corners and lay full and heavy at the centers. Her cheeks were red from the wind, her eyes sparkly wet and shiny.

Jack took in a long, deep breath and let it slowly out; somewhere inside him a sharp pain came and went. He was fifty-four. She couldn't be over twenty. Sometimes a man came face to face with what he might have been in this life, with what he might have possessed. It hurt, whenever this happened.

"Come on, Jackson, consarn it. The whiskey, man, the whiskey. We're froze to the bones and you stand there . . . Oh, excuse me. I forgot my cussed manners. This here is Miss Beverly Shafter. Miss Bev Shafter this here is Mister Jackson Miggs."

Jack gallantly nodded. He was old enough to be concerned about this slip of a girl being in the wild, rough, and lawless Ute Peak country, yet still young enough to feel the tug of her uncommon beauty.

She said: "All the way up and over the rim Frank's been telling me about you, Mister Miggs. About the time you outwrestled a bear. About the time the Utes caught you poaching their trapping streams and tied you with rawhide ropes . . . how you raised your arms, took a big breath, and burst every rope they had on you, then challenged any two of them at a time, and, after beating eight of them, how they let you go and called you a Dakota." She paused.

Miggs swiveled his gaze to Frank McCoy and wagged his head. "Don't you always believe Frank," he said. "Little lady, Frank McCoy's the longest-legged horse thief and the biggest liar between here and Kingdom Come."

The girl moved closer to the stove. She said from smiling, knowledgeable eyes: "He's also thirsty, Mister Miggs."

She was quietly laughing at Jack's old fashionedness and he knew it, so he brought out the earthenware jug, gravely handed it to McCoy, and settled his dead-level eyes once more upon Beverly Shafter.

"One time, many years back, I knew a man named Shafter. That was maybe before you were born, though. He trapped the uplands and drove freight in the summers. Sometimes he scouted for the Army, too, and, the way I heard it, that's what finally got him . . . scouting for the Army, I mean. Of course that was some years back when the Indians were still playing Old Nick up in here."

The girl's gray eyes lost their smile slowly when she said: "Whatever happened to him, Mister Miggs?"

"Well," said Jack, accepting the jug back from Frank McCoy, "I can't say for certain, little lady, but Hyatt Tolman, a cattleman from southward down around the Pagosa country, come onto the skeleton of a man sitting with his back to a big fir tree about fifteen, eighteen years back when he was hunting stray cattle in the back country." Jack paused to point up where an old, rusty long rifle lay across two whittled pegs along a beam rafter.

"Tolman brought back that musket. It was lying across the skeleton's lap. That was Jedediah Shafter's gun, little lady. I hunted and trapped and camped with him enough times to know it on sight." Jack dropped his big hand back to his side. "Well, the following spring I went up where Tolman told me he'd found the skeleton, but there wasn't anything left. I expect the cougars and wolves and what-not packed it all off during the winter to gnaw on. I did find a piece of a buckskin Ute hunting shirt, but that was all."

CHAPTER
TWO

They sat at Jackson Miggs's hand-made table, the three of them, two rough, graying men and the lovely girl, listening to scrabbling wind fingers worrying the outside rafter ends, and talked. For Miggs it had been a long, silent winter. He wanted to hear all the settlement news, but as this memorable day began to haze over with shadows from that towering monolith of northwestward granite, Ute Peak, and daylight began gradually to become a blue-gray blur, Miggs rose up, saying to McCoy: "Let's tend to the horses and supplies, Frank, and Miss Bev can make up supper if she's of a mind to."

This was a signal. McCoy recognized it as such and arose. Miggs smiled at the girl. "There's an elk haunch hanging out back under the eaves," he said, "and there's baking powder and flour in those drawers by the sink if you're of a mind to make biscuits. But the coffee, well, I ran out of coffee sometime back."

She smiled up at him. "Are you sure you don't mind?" she asked. "I've been told bachelors don't like women in their kitchens."

"Mind? Why, Miss Beverly, you're just about the nicest thing that's happened to me in twenty years. I don't mind at all."

Outside, Frank McCoy stood off a little distance looking up with his head tilted, watching sunlight's last golden spikes driving down hard into that pink snow field atop Ute Peak miles away. He heard Miggs come up and halt beside him, but he did not lower his head.

"That Shafter you told her about," he said quietly. "Jack, that was her paw."

"What? No, it couldn't have been, Frank. Why, old Jedediah Shafter never would've married a woman."

"He never did marry one," said McCoy, still squinting at that soft saffron overhead. "But he was her paw nonetheless." Finally McCoy dropped his head, swung it, and said: "Tell me something . . . it's been plaguing me all the way up here. Just what kind of a man was Jedediah Shafter, anyway?"

Jack looked over his shoulder. He muttered: "Come on . . . bring your horses to the corral. I'd rather not talk this close to the house."

While they were offsaddling, turning the animals loose up a grassy box cañon that required only three peeled-log poles across the open end to keep the beasts imprisoned, Jackson Miggs told Frank McCoy about Jedediah Shafter.

"He was a bull elk, Frank. I've seen him raise the yell and wade into the Ute war parties like he was crazy. I've also been with him when he'd cheat an old squaw out of her eyeballs, then get her drunk and steal her iron pots. Jed never had any use for females whether they were doe elk or squaw Indians. He lived hard, trapped good, fought like a she-bear, and I've always had a sneaking suspicion that he just didn't sit down

12

with his back to that tree and up and die like Tolman said he found him."

"No?"

"No. Jed just wasn't put here to die like an old squaw in the peaceful forest. No siree, he wasn't. That's why I made the trip up there to look at his carcass. I figured Tolman might've overlooked a bullet hole."

"Did he?"

"I don't know. Like I said in the cabin, Frank, by the time I got up there, wasn't enough left of Jed to tuck into the ground, but that's about right, too. Men like Jed Shafter don't die, really, they just sort of disappear. Maybe the Ghost Rider comes for 'em. Maybe . . ."

"That's Ute talk, Jack. You know better. But tell me . . . why would them soldiers he was scouting for shoot him?"

"Not the soldiers, Frank. Hell's bells, the soldiers couldn't have tracked a man like Jed Shafter. Indians."

"Indians shot him?"

"Utes. I'm not saying they did because I don't know. But they had reasons to try to, believe me about that."

"Why?"

But Jackson had said all he meant to say on that score. He walked over where McCoy was finished with hanging his rigs from some low limbs where night varmints wouldn't chew them to pieces looking for salt, and stood a while gazing down where smoke stood straight up from the chimney.

"Why did you bring her up here, Frank? What's she to you?"

"Her maw died in the winter. I knew her fairly well but she never once told me about Jed Shafter, and that's odd, too, because I . . ."

"Why did you bring her up here, Frank?"

"I'm trying to tell you, dog-gone it."

"Never mind her mother. I can guess about *that* from knowing Jed."

"Well, hell, Jackson," retorted McCoy a trifle sharply, his bushy brows rolling downward and inward a little. "She was plumb alone and being as pretty as she is and all, there were some cowmen wanted her to go to work in one of the Laramie dance halls. To tell you the truth, Jack, I didn't know what to do with her. I hung back starting into the mountains a week as it was. Then I figured I'd bring her along, try to figure out something on the way, and take her back out with me when I go."

Miggs turned, considered his old friend for a while, then said: "You aren't going to stay in and hunt this summer, Jack?"

"How can I, with her?" McCoy shook his shaggy head. "I tell you, Jack, it's a real problem."

They stood there in gathering gloom with that enormous peak off on Jackson Miggs's left, looking faintly disturbed, faintly perplexed as their kind sometimes look when, out of their own element where everything that can happen can be roughly coped with, they were as lost and helpless and naïve as lonely, unencumbered men can be.

Finally though, Frank McCoy said slyly, watching Miggs from the corner of one eye: "She sure can cook good. Even better'n her maw, and that's saying a lot

14

because her maw kept house for me for close to seven years, Jack."

"You never mentioned the girl."

McCoy shrugged. "It wasn't important. She was just a runny-nosed danged kid."

"You never told me the woman was Jed Shafter's woman, either."

"I never thought she was *that* Shafter's woman. There's a big family of Shafters out by Laramie, Jack. I always sort of figured she was one of that bunch. Not that I ever cared, nor even asked her. And for a fact she sure never told me."

"What'd she died of, Frank?"

Another shrug. "Lung fever, I reckon. She used to hack some now and then. I don't rightly know. You see, I was over on Green River doing a little horse trading and what-not most of last winter. Wasn't home much." McCoy ran a rough hand over his whiskery face. He was a lean-faced, long, thin man roughly as old as Miggs was, but he had an air of cunning to him that Miggs entirely lacked.

"Like I said though, Jackson, she's one hell of a fine cook."

Miggs swung half around, his face — what could be seen of it between nose and forehead — puckered up. "Oh, no, you don't," he growled. "You don't leave her with me as a housekeeper, Frank McCoy, dog-gone you."

"Who said anything about leaving her with you?" protested McCoy, looking astonished at such a suggestion, looking big-eyed and slack-jawed. "Why, where'd you ever get such . . . ?"

"Dog-gone you, Frank. You shouldn't have even brought her up here."

"I told you, damn it all, I had no choice. You figure I should've left her down there for those stinking cowmen to paw and maul?"

Jackson Miggs stood upon his wide-spread, mighty legs looking from McCoy back down toward his cabin, where a warm, pleasant yellow glow of lamplight spilled out a window and fell upon the wind-scourged soggy earth. There was something totally unfamiliar stirring within him. He could neither dodge it nor define it.

"That frying meat sure smells fine," murmured McCoy, coiling a rope, holding it at his side, and waiting for his host to move out toward the cabin. "I'm hungrier'n a starved bear."

They moved out side-by-side. The wind was dying out. It was losing some of its bluster and most of its solid strength. A big pewter disc floated serenely up from behind Ute Peak. As they neared the squat log cabin McCoy looked back at that moon and said: "A man can get his share of elk on a night like this, Jack. Remember, nine, ten years back when those gold hunters come up here and we sold 'em deer meat for elk and they didn't know the difference?"

Miggs paused outside the cabin also to view that big old moon and how it lay its silvery light over everything making the constant hush seem deeper.

"I remember a lot of those big moons," he mused. "Good ones and bad ones." He came down out of his

16

reverie abruptly, grabbed for the drawstring, and said: "Let's eat, Frank."

The girl had scrubbed up and combed her raven's wing tumble of wavy, thick hair. She seemed just as small to Jack but wiser now than she'd seemed an hour before. Wiser because she'd laid the food out exactly as a much older woman would have done, and wiser, too, because she looked straight into Jack's eyes with the old wisdom of womankind, half understanding, half challenging.

He could see her paw in her, too. He guessed the other part he saw, and did not recognize, must have come from her maw.

She said to Miggs: "Do you want to shave now?"

It startled him. He stood there, gazing down at her as though from an immense height, which was a way he had when something caught him unawares.

"Because if you do, I put water on to boil and scrubbed the wash basin . . . and . . . Frank brought you a new razor."

McCoy looked up from over by the stove. There was a sly look to his glance. He looked down, though, and, instead of speaking, began stuffing shag tobacco into a little stubby old pipe he always had with him.

"Now?" said Jack, fingering his big beard. "Before supper?"

She smiled up into his eyes, her face turning girlish, turning sweet. "There's plenty of time, Mister Miggs."

McCoy lit up, puffed furiously, then removed his pipe to say: "Sure, Jack, you got plenty of time. Besides" — Frank chuckled deep down — "hasn't anyone, including you, seen your ugly face since last September."

Frank drew something long-handled and shiny from an inner pocket, solemnly laid it over upon the washstand, and returned to his position by the stove, puffing away. The girl went back to her stove where elk haunch slabs sizzled.

Jack went to the basin, tucked under his shirt collar, and minutely examined the new razor. "Mighty fine," he said over his shoulder. "Thanks, Frank. It's a mighty fine piece of steel."

He did not want to shave and it had nothing whatsoever to do with delaying his supper. He had never before in his lifetime shaved before a female and it seemed downright indecent to do so now. Over across the room he could see McCoy standing there, grinning like an egg-sucking skunk because Frank knew exactly why he was stalling.

Beverly brought over the hot water, poured it, and went back to her frying meat. Jack dipped in cold water, tested it with a spatulate forefinger, sighed, and took down his shaving mug, shears, and comb. Every winter he let his beard grow for protection against the fierce cold and every spring he shaved it off — and for two weeks afterward he suffered every time a cold wind blew, the skin pink, tender, and unbelievably sensitive.

Frank said: "From the north rim we saw a herd coming up, Jack. It looked like maybe Tolman."

"Too early for him," replied Miggs, working determinedly with the shears first, letting great

18

swatches of hair fall floorward. "Hyatt won't be in for another month."

"Well, it was someone and they had a pretty big bunch of cattle."

"Coming on from Pagosa?"

"Looked like. Pretty dog-goned early, isn't it?"

"Yes. Normally no one's in this early. But this year it'll be all right. Won't be any more blizzards from now on."

McCoy ran this through his mind and agreed with it by nodding his head up and down.

At the stove Beverly Shafter said: "It's ready whenever you two are."

CHAPTER
THREE

Jack and Frank took three bearskins and two Hudson's Bay wool blankets apiece and went outside to sleep near the horses that first night, but the next day they made a partition across one end of Miggs's large, single-room log house for Beverly Shafter's cot and after that they'd bank the stove and sleep warm and private.

For three days they went crevice mining for gold, which was one of their summertime occupations. It had never netted them a whole lot but it was good to be out where the lupines were beginning to grow again, and the columbine, not to mention that deep down sunlight that beat with increasing warmth across their backs.

Then they went hunting, which was for both of them more than hunting for meat; it was a release of the spirit to men cooped up too long by thirty-below temperatures and ten-foot snowdrifts. They went out clad in moccasins, armed, and coated in response to a powerful inner urge, for this primordial call was the last vestige in civilized man of what he had once been.

They knew the elk grounds, the secret meadows, and tree-girted upland parks where snow-water freshets roared, white and bitterly cold, down through the first showings of rich green grass.

It was toward the end of their second day out that Jackson, cleaning sage hens they'd ground-sluiced, squatted close by Frank's quickening supper fire and said: "What'll become of her, Frank?"

McCoy showed no surprise. Neither of them had mentioned Beverly since leaving the cabin, but McCoy knew Jackson Miggs. Frank was by instinct a trader; he had every cunning, raffish propensity traders possessed, including the essential one that made him habitually read men.

"Someday a young buck'll come along," he replied, breaking twigs for the fire. "They always do, you know."

"Not up in here they don't. When you leaving to take her back?"

Frank held his hands over the fire and shrugged. "Next week maybe. The week after. You don't care when, do you? This sure beats doing our own cooking and washing, Jack."

"For us, yes, but I wasn't thinking of us. Can't be much fun for her . . . tending two old shag backs. Cooking and all the rest, without getting out much."

Jack finished with the sage hens, handed them to Frank on a thick green willow to be balanced upon rocks over the fire, and said: "She might like it at that. She's Jed Shafter's girl."

McCoy made the spit and began turning it. As he watched the hens cook, he said musingly: "You know, I always wanted kids of my own. That's a funny thing for a loner to want, isn't it?"

21

"No," said Miggs slowly, gazing down into the coals. "I don't think so, Frank. A man's got more purpose in life than just hunting and filling his belly all the time. The trouble is . . ."

"Yeah?"

Jackson Miggs drew in a deep breath and audibly let it out. "Well, it takes time to do all the things a man ought to do, and if a feller's busy all his waking hours just keeping alive, he doesn't have much time for . . . other things."

"Shafter made the time, Jack."

McCoy made a wry face. "Now you're talking about something altogether different and you know it. That used to be the Indian way. You came back from a raid or a hunt, sat around putting on tallow, filling out all the shrunken places of your gut, then you rode off again, leaving behind a squaw carrying your child, but that's not what you're talking about at all."

"No," murmured Frank McCoy, satisfied that he'd learned what he'd initially set out to learn. Jackson Miggs wasn't thinking of Beverly Shafter as a woman, he was considering her welfare, her future, her happiness. In short, Jackson was thinking paternally of Jed Shafter's girl and that was succinctly, precisely why Frank had brought her into the uplands with him.

He hadn't lied a whole lot to Jackson. He *had*, however, known she was Jedediah Shafter's child, and he *had* known what to do with her after her maw died — bring her to Miggs. A lonely man in his late middle years, after a winter of separation, was invariably hungry for the company of others. Frank knew all these things and he also knew, or thought he knew, something else. The older Miggs got, the more money he cached away each year, the less survival mattered, and the more he wished for more out of life in these sundown years.

"It's hard on youngsters nowadays," said Miggs as McCoy removed the golden brown, plump hens from their charred willow stick. "It used to be folks clove together . . . looked out for one another."

"That's the truth," agreed McCoy solemnly. "Watch out, that danged bird's hot."

They ate with shadows crowding up close to their little fire, with their squatting silhouettes projected against the hushed, giant tree trunks around them. Above lofty treetops a purple sky embellished with ice-cold, little flickering lights was night shadowed and velvety.

"I expect it's especially hard on young girls."

"Pretty ones like her, anyway. Why, Jack, you should've seen how those cowmen come a-rutting." McCoy ate, wiped grease from his chin, wagged his head, and said: "I didn't know what to do." And this was the truth; he hadn't known, until he'd thought of Miggs. "But I'll take her back next week and see if I can't find some widow woman or suchlike to leave her with. Then I'll go on over to Cheyenne and maybe hire out driving freight for . . ."

"Let's head back in the morning," interrupted Miggs, his face reflecting an inner decision. "We'll pick up some meat on the way down, Frank."

"All right."

"And clean up around the cabin . . . take her mining with us. I know some pockets in the rocks where she can scrape out twenty, thirty dollars in flake gold." Miggs smiled up around his dead-level gray eyes. "I can see her now . . . she'll be tickled as all get-out, finding her very own gold, Frank."

McCoy smiled. He chuckled deep down. His glance was cunning but it was also vastly relieved. "She sure will," he agreed.

"Unless you feel you got to take her back, Frank."

McCoy almost dropped his sage hen. His eyes grew large, grew round. "No," he blurted, then checked himself. "Don't have to go back at all, Jack. Hell, I don't like driving freight . . . eating dust all day and cold beans at sundown. No, you know how it is with me, Jack. If I can scrape out a hundred, a hundred and fifty dollars in flake gold between now and September, I'm plumb satisfied."

They banked their fire, rolled into their blankets, and lay back for a long time, silent. There was, to Jackson Miggs, an ancient oneness to the feel of earth and pine needles against his skin. There was an old, old promise, too, in that overhead purple tapestry above stiff treetops where the serene moon rode and those winking, aloof stars faintly flickered.

This was his kind of life. Lying like this in the womb of night surrounded by ageless mountains. Sometimes, in a man's youth, he thought for a time of other things. Of a woman's soft roundness perhaps and a family. But youth was a hurrying time and in the early manhood of Jackson Miggs there had been few women, indeed,

24

unless one considered Ute squaws, which he never had considered.

But no matter how fast a man hurried, life hurried past even faster until, like now, he was on the sundown side of fifty with a world of great memories — but also with an emptiness. There was no one now he could share those recollections with.

"Frank?"

"Yeah?"

"How old is she?"

McCoy brought up a hand, rubbed his nose, and screwed up his face. "I'd say eighteen. Maybe nineteen. No older, though."

"She seems older," mused Jackson Miggs in a detached tone of voice. He was thinking of how she'd boldly met his gaze, and softly smiled at him. Did they really mature at eighteen or nineteen? It was so awfully young. Yes, he told himself, they must, for she was a full woman. She'd had that ancient wisdom in her eyes, a knowledge of what life was. He sighed.

"Frank?"

"What?"

"Can she read and write?"

McCoy raised up a tousled head, squinted across the coals, and said: "Of course she can. Nowadays they all go to school, even girls."

"Times change, don't they?"

Frank didn't answer. He dropped back down, burrowed into his blankets, and heaved up onto one side. Somewhere nearby a horned owl hooted.

Miggs's loosening thoughts touched here and there in aimlessness until they closed down upon some recollections of her father. Jed had been a crafty, fearless, rough, brash man. He was the kind they worked up legends about, but that was the same kind other men, the ones who intimately knew, kept silent about, because for every legend there were other things best left unsaid.

The laudanum incident, for example. He and Jed had been trapping up around the Idaho country years back. Jed had gotten a bad tooth so they went down to Fort Hall, bought a big bottle of laudanum, and went back to the streams with it. Jed's toothache left eventually and they had a quart of laudanum left. Some Crows had come to camp one day, four of them on their way to the fort with their baled wintertime catch, $4,400 worth of prime skins. Jed had tried to trade them out of the furs with no success. He tried gambling, and lost half a bale of his own skins, instead. He then told them the laudanum was liquor, gave each Indian a tin cup of the stuff, and, when they'd toppled over unconscious afterward, Jed had loaded up all the furs and made a run for Fort Hall. Fortunately for Jackson Miggs, he had awakened before dawn, while the Crows were still unconscious. He figured out what Jed had done, and also made haste out of that country.

He didn't see Jed Shafter for three winters after that escapade, but, when they eventually did meet, Jed had thrown back his head and roared with laughter, saying he'd always wondered who awakened first, but now he knew, because, if the Crows had, Miggs's scalp lock would now be hanging from a Crow coup stick.

There were other things to be recalled, also, but Miggs pushed them out of his mind. He could imagine how Jed had gotten his daughter. He thought now that it was entirely possible Jed hadn't ever known he had a daughter, for Jed Shafter was like that. He was a composite of man and mountain lion, renegade and boon companion.

He shifted in his blankets. Well, thirty years back they were all more or less like that. He had been no saint himself, so he wasn't condemning Jed. But whether Jed ever knew it or not, he *did* have a daughter, and now she was alone.

Jackson Miggs was also alone.

Odd. He'd had strong leanings toward a family once, long, long ago. A hundred battles and maybe three, four dozen summers past, and now, past fifty years of age, here he was, still alone, and *she* was here, too, alone.

He blinked, gazed solemnly at those far-away stars. Odd how things worked out. Jedediah Shafter's girl without a father and Jackson Miggs without a family — a daughter.

That's what that pain had been inside him. He could define it now. Part sadness for what might have been and was not, part wistfulness, part sorrow.

"Frank?"

"*Hmmm.* What?"

"Oh. I didn't know you were asleep."

Frank's answer came back, muffled and indignant. "Well, now, just what in hell do you think I do when I roll up in my blankets and lie down?"

"Good night."

"*Humph!*"

Miggs moved restlessly. He was wide awake, wider awake this night than he'd been in years. But she wasn't a child, he mused. A child offered no insurmountable problems; you gave them shiny things to please them. What did you give an eighteen- or nineteen-year-old girl-woman?

Now stark reality came to plague Miggs. He'd let wistfulness and sentimentality run away with him. She was a grown girl. He became uneasy. More than that, she was at a marrying age. She wouldn't want to stay hidden under Ute Peak. More than likely she'd want to be around people more like herself, younger people.

Panic began to stir to life in Miggs. She'd leave. She'd go back down to the cow towns. He knew enough of those places to understand what could happen down there. How, then, to prevent it?

Maybe, if he and Frank worked at it hard enough, they could keep her happy and occupied at least during the summertime. Like going out crevice mining with them. Hunting, too, and they could take her to some secret lakes where trout were near as long as a man's arm.

That would please her and give Miggs time enough to ponder this other thing. He was thrilled with these ideas until it occurred to him that perhaps young girls didn't care about hunting and fishing.

He raised up suddenly, propped his shaggy head upon one thick hand, and gazed over where McCoy was effortlessly slumbering. Frank would know. After all, he'd known her since childhood.

"Frank? Oh, Frank?"

He got no reply at all this time. He dropped back down. He'd ask McCoy in the morning. He tried once more to sleep. It was no good. He had suddenly come upon something in these late years that entirely absorbed him, closing out everything else. It fastened itself upon him with a fierceness he'd never before felt for anything.

CHAPTER
FOUR

They left the uplands with day's first strong light and went angling downward toward the meadow country southeast of Ute Peak.

When they were leaving the last rim before descending to what was known as Frenchman's Flat, some six or seven miles from the log house in its own little green park, Jack halted, settled his rifle butt at his feet, and, while leaning upon the gun, jutted his chin westward toward the forested fringe of dark trees beyond the clearing of Frenchman's Flat.

"There's that herd you saw a week back," he said to Frank McCoy. "Coming out of the trees yonder."

McCoy squinted over where dark-hided cattle were mincing forward, testing the air and uncertainly shaking their wicked horns, and said: "Strangers to the country, those cattle. Wouldn't be Hyatt Tolman's, would they?"

"No. All Durhams. Never saw them before."

"See any riders with 'em?"

Miggs shook his head. He stood for a long time, watching the cattle push on out into the dewy grass. They were good cattle, had wintered well, and had a good start on picking up weight. Even the bulls looked good, which was not ordinarily the case with critters that had wintered in the lowlands where lice gaunted them up and sloughed off their hair in places.

"No calves," observed Frank. "Say, Jack, wonder whose cattle they are? He must be a pretty fair cowman. Probably one of those fellers who keeps the bulls out so's the calves won't drop before the feeds up strong."

Miggs said nothing. He'd never seen those animals before, and, while he agreed with what McCoy had just said, he wasn't thinking so much of the cattle as he was of the fact that new herds in the Ute Peak country meant that somewhere in the lowlands another cowman had been crowded out.

"Someday," he ultimately said, taking up his rifle and cradling it in one arm, "there'll be people thicker'n hair on a dog's back in these mountains."

"Tolman won't like it, when that day arrives."

Miggs looked around. "Tolman," he said, and grunted. "Tolman's as big a trespasser as this feller is, as far as I'm concerned. Well, come on."

They struck a familiar watershed, passed down it as silent as phantoms, stepped along to the thinning trees surrounding a grassy park where sunlight shone golden, and there saw what they'd been hoping to see — seven big elk.

The tree Jackson Miggs kneeled beside for his rifle rest was scarred as tall as a man's head from big animals rubbing their horns upon it. Frank also kneeled, but he made no move to lift his rifle. Instead he quietly said: "That blue cow, Jack. She's not with young, likely barren, and she's the fattest."

Jack froze, squeezed his trigger, the blue cow elk went down as though pole-axed, and the rest of the band broke frantically for cover on across the glade.

McCoy stood up, spat, hitched at his trousers, and started forward. As he passed Miggs, he said carelessly: "We should've brought a horse along. She's almighty big for us to bone out and pack back."

Jack remained where he was out of habit until he'd reloaded, then he also stepped into the clearing. He hadn't proceeded five feet before, on across the way, a big, bearded man jumped angrily into sight, threw up a saddle gun, and let off a shot over Frank McCoy's head. This big stranger swore in a thundering voice.

Frank fell like a stone, rolled frantically into a little depression, and looked out, his face showing purest astonishment. The thing had occurred so entirely unexpectedly that McCoy didn't have time for anger; that would come later.

But Miggs's reaction was altogether different. He operated quite by instinct when that high shot exploded. He could have been thirty years younger with a Ute war party over there in the trees. He dropped to one knee, whipped up his rifle, and caught that furious, bearded man in his sights, tugged off a shot, jumped sideways, and began reloading. He scarcely waited to see whether he'd scored or not.

He had. The big, angry man went sideways, striking one tree, caroming off that one to strike a second tree, then drop, threshing, into the grass, his bellowing as loud and wrathful as a bear's bellowing would have been.

Frank snaked his way back to Miggs, scuttled behind a tree, and slowly straightened up. Jack got back to him with his reloaded weapon and his iron-hard expression. Together they watched that big man throw himself around, beating a retreat. They heard his sizzling epithets, too, and finally they heard horsemen charging recklessly down the yonder slope, calling to the bearded man.

"Cowboys," said McCoy. "Jack, we winged us a damned cowboy."

Frank was wrong. They had gotten themselves a *cowman*, not a cowboy. The owner of a herd, not a rider.

"Hey, over there," came a voice from back in the yonder trees. "What the hell you figure you're doin', shootin' folks?"

McCoy and Miggs exchanged a look. Neither answered that call but both glided deeper into the easterly forest. That was too old a trick to catch Frank McCoy or Jackson Miggs, that calling out to hold someone's attention while others slipped around and came up behind them.

It was riders. They heard them passing softly over beds of pine needles, rein chains and spur rowels jangling.

Frank made a wry face. "Nowadays," he murmured to Jack, "men just don't use their heads at all, riding around here making all that noise."

Jack grunted, lifted a massive arm, and pointed to a shadowy place among the trees where three horsemen appeared, halted to scrutinize the way ahead, then eased out their animals again, coming on steadily with carbines athwart their saddle swells.

That yelling man across the glade kept up his denunciation. He demanded to know who Miggs and McCoy were, what business had they in these mountains. He also called them some uncomplimentary names, all as a screen so that his friends on horseback could get close enough either to capture or shoot them.

It didn't work out that way, though. When those three cowboys halted again, sniffing pungent black powder stench at the site where Jack had fired, a long-legged, cadaverous wraith appeared upon their right, and, from behind, a massive, squat phantom appeared upon their left, long-barreled rifle up and ready.

"Throw down those carbines," said Jackson Miggs quietly. "Never mind looking around, just dump those guns."

The cowboys obeyed. They exchanged looks of helplessness. Neither the man who had spoken to them nor the other man they knew was with him were in sight.

"Now those pistols."

The handguns also dropped onto spongy pine needles.

Jackson Miggs stepped into full view. He went around until the cowboys could plainly see him, lowered his rifle to the crook of one arm, and considered those youthful, whiskery faces, saw none that he knew, and said: "How bad's that feller hurt over there?"

The riders did not forget McCoy. As one answered Miggs, another one craned his neck around for a sighting of the gun they knew perfectly well was covering them from behind. The third cowboy slowly raised a gloved hand, slowly rubbed his stubbled jaw, and gradually began to grin.

"He'll live," said a dark-eyed, lean, and quick-looking man. "You cut through the meat atop his shoulder and knocked him down, but it ain't a truly serious hurt."

"That's too bad," said Jack, gazing upon those young mounted men, his voice quiet and easy sounding. "It was kind of a quick shot but I aimed to bust his gun arm."

"Mister," said the dark, lean rider, "you killed his horse with that wild shot you took at that cow elk."

"I see. That's what brought him out like that, cussing and shooting. Well, I'm sorry about the horse, young man, but you see I had no idea at all anyone was within five miles of me up in here."

"You could've sung out," snapped another cowboy.

Jack looked at this one. He didn't seem to be over eighteen or nineteen years old. He had the hot intolerance of youth up in his eyes like a banner.

"I could've," assented Miggs, "but, sonny, I was after meat."

"Who are you an' why don't your pardner come out where we can see him? You fellers afraid we might be the law?"

Jack kept studying that hot-headed younger man. The other two, in their late twenties, quiet now, were absorbed in studying Miggs's moccasin-clad feet, his long-barreled old-time rifle, and the little swatch of coarse black hair that dangled from the bottom of his skinning knife sheath.

Jack grounded his gun, leaned on it, and looked the younger man up and down before saying: "Sonny, I see someone forgot to teach you manners. I've got the gun, not you, so I'll ask questions, and you . . . well . . . you just keep your mouth shut."

Jack waited, watching that youthful face fill with dark blood.

But when the cowboy would have spoken back sharply, the stockier man on his right, half grinning, said carelessly: "Shut up, kid. Like the feller says . . . he's got the gun." This man's gaze downward at Jackson Miggs showed steely and fearless. "He's young," this man said in that easy, warm way he had of carelessly speaking. "The feller you winged is Denver Holt. We ride for him. We brought the Holt cattle up here because the boss had heard the feed had come on early and was strong."

"Where you from, mister?"

"The Green River country."

"You've come a long way."

The cowboy shrugged. "Not really. We wintered this bunch on the Laramie plains. The home ranch is at Green River."

"Frank," Miggs called quietly, and McCoy stepped out into view, lowered his rifle, and sauntered over to halt beside Jack, looking challengingly upward. Then Miggs said to that rider with the lop-sided little grin: "A cowman from the Pagosa country usually ranges this country hereabouts in the summertime, mister. Hyatt Tolman. Maybe you've heard of him."

"Nope. We're strangers hereabouts, old-timer."

"Well, there's a lot of good grass on westward. Just so's Tolman's herd and yours don't get mixed up, it might be best if you drifted your stock westerly."

"Sure," said the cowboy. "I'll tell Mister Holt. Mind if I ask a question, seein' that you've still got the gun, an' all?"

Jack nodded his head.

"Do you fellers live up here?"

"About four miles south," Jackson replied. "Where are you fellers camped?"

The cowboy flagged westerly with one gloved hand, broadened his lop-sided grin, and said with a hard twinkle: "These consarned trees all look alike to me. About all I can tell you is that our camp's on the site of some old Indian *rancheria* in a big valley under that big peak yonder."

Jack nodded. "I know the place," he murmured, then, in a stronger tone: "Tell Mister Holt I didn't know he was yonder in the trees or I wouldn't have shot. If there's anything I can do for him . . ."

"He's comin' across the glade," interrupted the hot-tempered youngest rider. "Tell him yourself, mister."

They all turned. There were two big men walking along out there in the bright morning light. One was a younger edition of the older, heavier man. Obviously they were father and son.

Denver Holt had a bloody tear in his woolen shirt and had no spring in his step, but he seemed otherwise little the worse for his creased shoulder. He was a large, raw-looking, fierce man with a gray-reddish beard, testy small eyes, and a hard jaw. The big man walking with him, carrying a Winchester loosely in his gloved right fist, was big-boned, too, and there was that same fierce flash to his gaze. Anger came out of those two, as they crossed the last hundred feet to where Miggs and McCoy stood, as solid as granite.

Miggs considered, muttered something to Frank, and, under the watching glance of these three unarmed cowboys, Frank faded back, glided around, and came down where the Holts entered the first tree fringe.

"Drop that gun," he ordered, cocked his own weapon to give solid weight to his words, and waited.

Big Denver Holt stopped, peered for some sight of McCoy, saw the others father back in shadow, could not locate Frank, and growled at his son. The Winchester fell into the grass.

McCoy stepped forth, wagged the Holts onward, and fell in behind them. In this manner the entire crew of Denver Holt was reunited.

Miggs, looking into those flinty, wrathful faces, put his dead-level gaze upon the eldest man and kept it there. He apologized for winging Holt, said he'd replace the shot horse, repeated what he'd earlier told Holt's men about Hyatt Tolman ranging this particular part of the uplands, then stopped speaking and stood there leaning upon his rifle, waiting.

The big cowman's son, whose name was Bert, ran a scornful gaze over those three unarmed mounted men. "Fine bunch," he snarled. "Three of you and you let these two old squawmen get the drop on you."

Miggs's gaze whipped across to the younger Holt. That squawman term pushed him to the edge of violence.

Denver Holt said: "I saw those elk, too. That's what I was doing . . . slippin' up on them . . . when you cut loose. Mister, after this, you'd better stay out of this part of the hills because my boys and I'll be up here. The next time you go huntin' somewhere else."

The arrogance of this order stung Frank McCoy. "You're the one that's trespassing!" he exclaimed. "You and those Durhams of yours. Jack here give you some good advice about hunting another place to graze 'em . . . and make your cow camp. I wouldn't be that nice. I'd just let Tolman find you in his stamping grounds."

"Would you now," growled the big, grizzled old cowman at Frank. "This is open country and free range. First come, first served. Your Hyatt Tolman'll have to find new range this year . . . not us." Holt's testy gaze whipped back to Jack. "As for you, feller, the next time you shoot at me, by God, you'd better aim straighter because I'll kill you. And I won't holler out like I did this time."

Jack's gaze turned smoky. He took up his rifle, laid it across one bent arm, jerked his head at Frank, and started off. McCoy, not as angry as Miggs was, and a

39

lot craftier, retreated slowly, placing each foot down behind him with care, keeping his eyes and his gun barrel upon those five silent, wooden-faced men back there. He didn't turn and go rushing downcountry after Miggs until he'd put a solid wall of trees between himself and Holt's crew. Then he struck a loose trot and jogged along until he came up with Miggs, who was pausing at a little trail-side spring to drink deeply of good cold water.

"That's a bunch for you," McCoy said, also kneeling to drink. "First time up in here and already they're giving orders."

"He was mad all right," replied Jack, rising up, flinging water off his chin. "That's why I walked away. I was getting mad, too. It was his shoulder, I reckon, Frank. That, and being taken like they were. We'll let him cool down a while. He'll probably be all right after he gets over this meeting."

CHAPTER
FIVE

They came across two buck deer a mile from the cabin, killed both, boned out the meat, and made shoulder packs of the hides. With this burden they returned to the cabin, arriving there with the last soft glow of dying day over everything.

Beverly was there to greet them, her eyes shining and her smile wide. She helped them hang the meat from the rounded back-roof beams to cool out. Neither Frank nor Jack mentioned the meeting with Denver Holt. They had almost forgotten about it themselves in fact. But Jack did say they meant to take her crevice mining with them two days later.

It was good to be back. It was always good to return with plenty of meat. They sat by the fireside after supper and talked. Frank had packed in enough shag tobacco to last both men a year, so they puffed their pipes, and, when Beverly asked Miggs about the father she'd never known, he sat there relaxed, gazing mistily into the fire, spinning great tales of Jedediah Shafter. Frank McCoy, over where dancing shadows alternately darkened and brightened his thin, raffish face, looked solemn everywhere but in the eyes, as he listened to Miggs carefully creating an image of Beverly's father for the girl that Frank strongly suspected was stretching the truth about as far as it could be stretched.

Later, when the two men went outside for a last look at the horses, he said to Miggs: "You handled that right well, Jack."

And Miggs, knowing what McCoy was referring to, said back: "What'd you expect a man to do . . . tell her the truth? Young folks got to believe their kin are a sight better'n most of them ever were. Particularly that pretty little lady in there." Jack leaned upon a peeled log, gazing up where the horses were dimly visible under a smoothly worn old moon. "It's sort of like religion," he mused. "When folks attribute virtue to something they powerfully admire, Frank, they just naturally try to copy that hero, and they become better people for the trying, although the object they worship maybe wasn't really very virtuous at all. You understand?"

"I understand you do a heap of thinking up in here by yourself all winter," retorted McCoy, not understanding at all. "Come on, let's get back. It's colder'n a witch's kiss out here."

They returned to the cabin. Beverly was already abed. She'd left the lamp turned low. This mellow, orange light softened every axe mark otherwise visible on the log walls; it gentled the crudity of the cabin and left only that feeling of pleasant warmth, of security that such uplands log houses possess.

Miggs and McCoy turned in. Frank dropped off with no more ritual than one rattling big sigh, but Jackson Miggs lay in his blankets for a long time wondering how he'd bring up the question of staying on, to the girl. He thought, too, of the things in his heart, but he was a patient, wise man. One learned to be patient and philosophical when one spent months cabin-bound in a world of endless hush and frigid whiteness.

He'd find a way and the place, somehow, to speak to her. This was only the second week she'd been in the Ute Peak country. There was a lot of time yet.

He fell asleep feeling wistful, feeling poignant, and feeling good inside. He had quite forgotten Denver Holt and Holt's big herd of Durham cattle.

In fact, only after they were down in the southern reaches, crevice mining, two days later, their camp established beside a clear-water pool where sunlight hammered golden sheets over the water, did he have occasion to remember Holt at all.

They had taught Beverly how to walk up the creeks with her hunting knife and a little buckskin bag, find fissures in the rocks where wintertime freshets had deposited silt in the cracks, and carefully, using the edge of her knife, uncover little gold deposits. She had been as thrilled and excited, as Jack had thought she would be, the first time she found a gold pocket all by herself. Watching her, he thought she must have been an unusually lively little girl, because now, as a big girl, she laughed and sparkled even when she fell once and cut her hand upon sharp creek-side stones.

They stayed at this camp for four days, going out separately each morning with their knives and little bags, crevice mining. On the fifth day, deciding they'd explored all the byways within a goodly radius of their present site, they decided around the campfire that the next morning they'd strike camp and move on westward where Frank and Jack knew of other creeks worth mining.

But before daylight of the fifth day Jack rolled out, pulled on his boots, took his rifle, and slipped out of camp without waking the others. He followed his sensitive nose a mile southward, as far as a juniper top out, and hunkered up there, awaiting first light to see whether or not his nose had played him false.

It hadn't. When the steely brightness widened, lightened, turned the downcountry eerily visible below where he sat cross-legged, waiting, he saw the distinct, far blur of moving cattle. It had been the scent of those animals that had roused him two hours earlier.

He sat there until, off in the far-away east, pale pink and milky yellow came on ahead of a nearly rising sun, giving back to the land the dimensional depth and solid substance that had been robbed by the nighttime.

The herd showed best where brush and trees backgrounded it because these were Herefordcross cattle, nearly all of them with dark red hides but with totally white or partially white faces. He knew these critters. It was late May now. A mite earlier than usual for Hyatt Tolman to be driving into the uplands, but those were unmistakably his animals.

Jack returned to camp. Bev had breakfast cooking. Frank was putting their packs back up into a tree so foraging varmints wouldn't find them while the three were out mining.

From back a little way among the gloomy trees Miggs halted to lean upon his rifle and watch the girl.

She worked at the breakfast fire, head down, every now and then jutting her underlip to blow upward at a coil of heavy black hair that swung low across her forehead. She had taken to the ways of camping like a duck takes to water. He told himself that it was in her naturally to do this, for whatever anyone had ever said about her father, one thing a man could say truthfully about him was that Jed Shafter was one of the best mountaineers ever put upon this earth.

He stepped out into full view, saw McCoy's and the girl's eyes rise to him, and said: "Tolman's coming. Just been down to see his cattle pushing up the trail."

McCoy finished securing the ropes where he'd jerked their packs up out of ground reach, went over, and eased down where Miggs had seated himself across from Beverly. When she had filled their tin cups with coffee and passed them over, she affectionately smiled at Jack.

Frank leaned over to whisper. "You'd best head Tolman off and tell him about that Holt outfit. I doubt if he'll want his heifers bred to those Durham bulls. He told us last summer he was trying to breed up into this white-faced breed and not back into the shorthorn line."

Jack nodded. "We'll take care of that. He won't be up here at the rate he's traveling now for another three hours."

Beverly saw them talking low, back and forth, but wisely let this go past. She gave them their plates, blew that shiny black curl upward, and said to Miggs: "Frank thinks I have forty dollars' worth of flake gold." She dropped her head a little to one side, twinkled a quick, girlish smile at Jack, and added: "This is the first money I ever had of my own. I think, when we go back, I'll buy you a new black hat at Laramie, and myself a long, flowing white dress."

Jack's hand grew still midway to his mouth. *When she went back . . . ?*

"Hey," protested McCoy, his thin, lined face creasing with mock indignation. "What about me? I brought you up here, remember."

"I'll never forget that," she said, her warm smile softening toward McCoy. "It's everything you said it was, and more, Frank. I could stay up in here forever. I never felt so good in my life, nor . . ." She broke off, narrowed her liquid dark eyes at McCoy, got a knowing, wise look, and said: "I'll buy you a case of Old Crow whiskey, Frank, and a brand-new red wool shirt."

Frank was placated but Jack said nothing and finished eating, after which the three of them went to the pool to scrub their utensils. There, Jack said: "Bev, the winters here are lonely and bitter cold. You wouldn't like it then."

"Winter's cold everywhere," she replied. "At least up in here the snow would be clean and the stillness good. In Laramie the snow is dirty . . . and so are the noises."

That was all either of them said on that subject. Beverly took her knife, her little poke, and went up where she'd located a promising crevice the evening before. She shot Jack and Frank a quick warm smile, leaving them standing together by the dying campfire.

46

As they watched her sturdy, small figure head up into the shadowy places, McCoy said: "Jack, it's a good thing there's only us two old gaffers to see her dressed in those tight doeskin pants and chalk-tanned Ute squaw blouse, for I swear she's just about the most likely looking female a man could ever lay eyes on."

Miggs began covering the campfire coals with the edge of one boot. After a while he said: "Frank, I'll be eternally damned if I can figure out how an old devil like Jed Shafter ever got himself a daughter as pretty and sweet as that little lady is."

McCoy smiled. "Why, Jackson, I heard you with my own ears explaining about how fine a feller her paw was just the other night."

Miggs looked over toward the gloomy cañon where Beverly had gone, looked back, and said: "Come on . . . let's go find Tolman."

They took their rifles, headed leisurely southward as far as that top out where Miggs had squatted earlier, and there halted to consider the sea of dark red backs below where Tolman's cattle were beginning to push upward along the game trails, streaming steadily northward. The older animals among that herd, bulls and cows, knew through some dim but persevering instinct, where they were going. The younger animals, mostly heifers, contentedly climbed along behind the older animals. If a few strayed, it made no difference. They had all the summer — up until the first frost in September — to find the others.

"Only three riders," said Frank, pointing far back where the calving cows, the footsore critters, and the oxen-paced big bulls trudged along. "Odd. Usually Tolman brings five, six men up with him."

Miggs, having already noticed this, had a plausible but incorrect explanation. "Hyatt isn't with those three, so I'd guess he's maybe off on a side trail somewhere with a rider or two. Maybe bringing on some cut-backs."

This satisfied McCoy. They stood up there, watching that big herd push on up toward them, breaking right and left around the granite precipice they stood upon.

"There's Fred Brian," said Miggs as the three riders converged and a broad-shouldered man in a black wool shirt to match his broad black hat gestured for the other two horsemen to break up — one to trail northward to the right of the cliff, the other cowboy to trail off to the left.

"He must still be Hyatt's range boss," mused Frank. "You know, I got the impression last summer when he visited the cabin that he wanted to strike out on his own."

Miggs nodded. Evidently he'd also gotten this impression, for he said: "They all do sometime or another. If they're any good, they do."

"Brian's a good cowman."

"Yeah. He's got more savvy at twenty-seven than you and I had, Frank. Otherwise, we'd have amounted to something other than a pair of old leftovers from another era."

"Wait a minute," protested McCoy. "You got more money cached in these mountains than Hyatt Tolman's got in the Pagosa bank, I'll bet."

48

"And you?" asked Miggs, with a smile. "What've you got, Frank, besides your health?"

"Hell's bells, that's enough isn't it? Tolman's got more money'n I've got, sure, but last summer he didn't look so good, did he?"

"No, he didn't. Come on. Fred's heading up this way."

CHAPTER
SIX

Fred Brian had been Hyatt Tolman's range boss since he'd been twenty-three years old. He was a powerful man just under six feet tall with a smooth, handsome, and sun-tanned face. He was a man other men instantly cottoned to, and down in Pagosa it hadn't always been men who'd found his company pleasant and welcome.

As he rode leisurely along now, making for the steepening rise into the upland, meadow country below Ute Peak, he trailed two pack horses fully loaded, and kept his experienced eyes upon the herd ahead, the stragglers near the tag end of that herd, and his two riders.

He did not anticipate meeting anyone for another five or six miles, so when Jackson Miggs and stringy Frank McCoy stepped forth beside the trail, Brian was surprised. He called a greeting to those two, grinned, and at once dismounted to pass over into forest shade and stand there hipshot, looking from one of the older men to the other.

"You're looking fit," he said by way of greeting to Miggs. "And, Frank, you're about like always . . . sort of leaned-down and tucked-up-looking."

McCoy smiled. He and Miggs shook hands with this powerful, confident younger man with that gun tied to his right leg and that thick auburn hair visible where he'd thumbed back his hat.

"Where's Hyatt?" Jackson Miggs asked, throwing a look back southward. "He's usually the first one up the trail."

Instead of replying immediately, Fred Brian fished a soiled, limp envelope from his pocket and pushed it out to Miggs. "For you," he said, and added nothing to those two words.

Jack took the envelope, opened it, smoothed out the letter that the envelope contained, read it, and afterward lifted perplexed, troubled eyes to the younger man.

"It's asking a lot, I know," murmured Brian, his gaze grave and heavy. "He thought you might do it, seeing you've been friends these past fifteen years or so."

"Do what?" asked McCoy, edging up closer, full of sudden interest, sudden curiosity. "What is it, Jack?"

Miggs ignored McCoy to reread that letter, his brows furrowing, his eyes turning solemn and troubled. He eventually said to Brian: "I'm no cattleman, Fred."

"The boys and I'll do whatever's got to be done," replied Hyatt Tolman's range boss. "I brought along plenty of grub and what-not to keep us going up in here for a while."

"You figure to stay all summer, Fred?"

Brian nodded. "Those are my orders, Jack." He kept watching Miggs.

McCoy screwed up his face. "What's wrong?" he demanded. "Say, has something happened to Tolman?"

"Flat on his back down at the ranch," said Brian, still watching Jackson Miggs. "Doctor says he'll be laid up for at least two months."

"What ails him?"

Brian shrugged, shot Frank a brief look, and returned to watching Jack, waiting for Miggs to make his decision. "There've been three doctors in this winter, Frank, and all three got a different notion of what's ailing him. About all they agree upon is that it's inside him . . . some kind of foul-up in his inner workings. Anyway, in that letter he sent Jackson, he's asked if maybe Jackson wouldn't sort of ramrod for him while the cattle are up here. Like I just said . . . any cow work that's got to be done, my two riders and I'll do. All he wants is for Jackson to sort of watch over the critters because he knows the mountains better'n anyone around." Brian paused, waited for Jack to speak, and, when Miggs did not, Brian said: "Well, how about it? He'll pay you foreman's wages, Jack."

"Fred," said Frank, sounding disgruntled, "we've got hunting and crevice mining to do and . . ." McCoy suddenly went silent, his eyes widening. "Hey," he said, giving Jack's elbow a bump, "you better tell him about that Holt outfit."

Miggs carefully folded the letter, one of the extremely few written communications he'd received in his lifetime, placed it back into its soiled envelope, and pushed the thing into a pocket.

52

"I'll help you all I can," he told Fred Brian. "I'd do that anyway, Fred, but not for money. Just for old times' sake. I'm right sorry to hear about old Hyatt, too. The first man you send back down to Pagosa, have him tell Hyatt we'll make out all right, the five of us."

"Sure," said Brian showing obvious relief.

"The *five* of us," croaked McCoy. "Brian here, his two riders, you . . . and who else, Jack?"

"You, of course," answered Miggs, twisting to look at McCoy.

"What about our mining and hunting?"

"We'll have time for those things."

"Sure you will," put in Fred Brian placatingly. "Frank, whatever you're short come fall, I'll make up to you in cash money."

McCoy's eyes craftily brightened at this. Jack saw that look and wagged his head back and forth. But he said nothing, only flagged on up the trail for Brian to follow after, and began walking ahead, back toward the campsite beside the clear-water pool.

Frank caught up with Jack when he was a hundred yards farther onward. He said: "Tolman must be pretty sick to ask you to oversee things for him."

"He must be," assented Miggs, strolling along with his head down and his bushy brows knit.

"Say, you forgot to mention to Brian about that other cow outfit up in here."

"I didn't forget, Frank. It's just that there's plenty of time to tell him, and right now we've got to figure something out."

"Yeah, how to get in our hunting and suchlike, while stewing about Tolman's cattle, too."

"No," contradicted Miggs. "No, Fred's capable of all that, and maybe any other summer helping Tolman out wouldn't be so hard. But this year'll be different. I can see that plain as day."

"Different, how?"

"Holt. You heard him, Frank, you saw him. He's right, too, about this being free country up under Ute Peak."

McCoy paced along turning all the implications behind Jackson Miggs's words over in his mind. He knew Hyatt Tolman and he also knew Tolman's range boss, Fred Brian. As Denver Holt and his son Bert were alike, so also were old man Tolman and his quiet-eyed range boss. There could be trouble brewing here. Frank swung a look at Miggs, saw Jack's thoughtful expression, and said no more.

Beverly was not at camp when they arrived there. In fact she didn't show up even after Fred Brian had come up with his two riders to offsaddle and lift down their laden *alforjas* from the pack animals. Not until one of the riders, a youthful, freckled, and snub-nosed man came walking back from the pool holding a silk scarf in his fingers and looking puzzled, did Jack explain about the girl, and even then he used a minimum of words, for that other thing was deeply on his mind.

He explained, finally, about the Holt herd as Brian and the others cooked up a midday bait of food.

Tolman's range boss looked displeased, but for a while he said nothing, only considered all that Miggs and McCoy told him, including the shooting of Denver Holt. Eventually he asked some questions concerning Holt's men and cattle, and sipped his black coffee in pensive silence.

When they had finished eating, Brian said across the fire to Miggs: "This is going to make it even tougher, Jackson. Hyatt will raise hell and prop it up with a big stick if, come next calving season, our cows and heifers come up with Durham calves. He's trying hard to breed out the Durham and breed in the Hereford."

"We talked on that," said Frank McCoy.

Fred paid Frank no heed. "That's how come us to fetch along that bunch of purebred white-face bulls, Jackson. Hyatt spent most of last winter getting those bulls. They're the best money can buy and they came all the way to Colorado from Kansas."

Miggs watched one of the cowboys make a smoke, light it, and exhale a small blue-gray cloud. "We can ride over and talk to Holt," he suggested, sounding a lot less than enthusiastic about the outcome of any such visit.

"You said you already told him this was Tolman's range, Jackson."

"That's right, Fred, but what else can we do?"

The smoking cowboy made a rough smile and said through exhaled smoke: "Round up their critters . . . 'specially their danged Durham bulls . . . and push 'em west a few dozen miles."

"You fellers better take a long look at this here Denver Holt and his crew, particularly that mean-looking son, before you try anything like that," put in Frank McCoy, "because I got a feeling the minute you commence chousing Holt's beef, you're going to think the sky fell on you."

"Like that, eh," murmured the freckle-faced, snub-nosed rider, his blue eyes brightening and hardening. "Well, for my part I never did like strangers ridin' up an' throwin' their weight around. What'd you say, Fred? We could likely find all this Holt's bulls by this time tomorrow if we got right on it."

But Brian shook his head, pushed up to his feet, looked out and around, and said to the red-faced rider: "When folks start making war talk, Red, they usually get trouble up to their ears. For now, you and Lex take the horses and packs on up to Jackson's cabin. The rest of us'll meet you there this evening."

Frank went out to help the cowboys saddle up and toss their diamond hitches on the pack beasts. Miggs remained near the fire with big Fred Brian. He sighted on the sun, guessed the time to be 11:00 a.m. or a little after, wondered idly when Beverly would return from her crevice mining, then had his thoughts intruded upon as Brian said: "Fine kettle of damned fish. I figured, once we got up in here with the cattle, our big troubles would be over."

"They may be over," said Jack. "No point in stewing until we've seen the Holts."

56

Brian looked over caustically and murmured: "You don't believe that, Jackson. Not after what you've been telling me about these Holts and their riders."

Miggs squinted out at the sun again. "Maybe I don't, but I'll tell you one thing, Fred. With you and me and Holt, I think there'll be a lot less chance of a flare-up than if Hyatt was here. He's too much like that Denver Holt."

"But he's trespassing, Jackson."

Miggs brought his squinted eyes down, fixed them sardonically upon Brian, and grunted. In his private opinion everyone who entered the uplands back country except the animals who lived here was trespassing. All he said, though, was: "Like Holt told me, Fred . . . it's open range."

Brian looked glum, perplexed. "I don't want trouble," he said. "If he just didn't have damned Durham bulls."

McCoy strolled back. The two cowboys were heading on up into the north trees with their charges. When they spoke to one another, their voices and words drifted back distinctly for a long time after they'd passed from sight of the three men still at the campsite.

"Well," said Frank McCoy, scuffing dirt over the coals underfoot, "when Bev comes on in with her poke of gold, we can head on up for the cabin."

Jack unconsciously looked at the sun again. "She must've found a good spot. It's close to high noon right now."

"She'll be along," said Frank carelessly, finishing with the fire. "Say, Fred, if you're going on, how about taking some of our stuff ahead to the cabin with you?"

Brian agreed to this, went for his rigged-out horse, led the animal back, and tied as much of the two men's effects as he could behind his cantle. He swung up over leather then, nodded, and started along after his cowboys.

When Brian was gone, McCoy eased down upon some dusty, soft earth, fixed Miggs with a shrewd eye, and said: "I can smell it, Jack."

"Smell what?"

"Trouble. It's got a smell all its own."

Miggs hunkered, looked once more at the overhead sky, and muttered: "I wish she'd come back. I'd like to get back home before dark tonight."

"She'll be along, stop your fretting. I've known Bev since she was knee-high to a grasshopper and never known her to get lost yet. She's got a built-in compass inside her skull. Must've got that from her old paw."

With Miggs hunkered there, solemn-faced and totally silent for a long enough time, Frank, turning drowsy under that unrelenting overhead sun, said conversationally: "Jack, what's Hyatt Tolman so dead set against Durham cattle for? I recollect the time when he had more brown cattle than anyone in the country."

Miggs shrugged. "He told me last summer these white-faced Herefords are the coming beef cattle. That Durhams go dry faster and don't shape up so well. But, Frank, I've been a trapper and hunter most of my life and one breed of cattle looks pretty much like any other breed to me . . . so long as they're the same color. I can tell you one thing . . . fat Durhams or these fat white-faces . . . after a long winter like we just lived through, eating elk and bear and deer, good fried beef sure is an agreeable change."

Frank grinned. It was the custom of these two, once the herds entered the uplands country, to practice on a modest scale what the former owners of this same land, the Ute Indians, had also done — they levied on Tolman and other ranchers for one fat steer each time the herds came up the trail. It was a good-natured asking and a good-natured giving, this ritual.

"I wish she'd hurry along," said Jack, a little annoyed as the sun began its westerly glide. "Dang it all."

CHAPTER
SEVEN

By 3:00p.m. Jack was more bothered by Beverly's absence than ever. While he associated no particular trouble with her absence, he did grumble to Frank McCoy about not being able to make it home before sundown now.

Frank was not concerned about the girl's absence, but he said: "You go along, Jack. I'll wait here and fetch Bev on home when she comes back from her mining. You ought to be at the clearing when Brian sets his camp up there, but I don't have to be, so go along with you."

Miggs hoisted the balance of their effects, took up his rifle, and went off through the upland forest, northbound. He walked with the short, steady, chopping gait of mountain men. He had two hours to make up if he meant to arrive back at his log house before dark.

The meadows were hazed over with afternoon sun glaze. Even in the forest's eternal gloom, the scents and shades were of burgeoning summertime. Where before there had been only dank earth or moldering mulch, now there were flowers of many kinds, colors as vivid, as tumultuous as springtime could make them. And that softly fragrant odor of running sap in the trees was good again, after months of bitter cold and steely days.

Miggs sensed rather than fully noticed these things. Ordinarily he looked keenly at each new sign of this life-giving season of the year. But this afternoon, walking swiftly along, trailing his rifle, and lightly packed, he saw but scarcely heeded all that strong beauty around him in its heady profusion.

Even after the reddening sun dropped away behind aloof Ute Peak, he did not entirely appreciate the long, quiet afterward hour when there was no sound anywhere, when the earth yielded up its cooling scents, and the overhead sky turned milky with pink streamers flowing down it from east to west.

The problem of just how to handle Denver Holt vexed Miggs. If he hadn't shot at that blue cow elk, he thought, things might in prospect be different. He wasn't at all sure about that, though; Denver Holt didn't look like a man who would give way to importunities.

But he *had* shot the cow elk, and he *had* winged Denver Holt.

He stepped out into the little glade where his log house sat upon the northwesterly end, and moved swingingly along toward a guttering campfire whose backdrop was the dark and bulky front of his own cabin.

Lex and Red Morton had the cow camp established next to Miggs's creek, but downstream from the house. Brian was not at once in sight but all their horses were, and the heavy packs, plus saddle rigs, carbines in scarred leather saddle boots, and other accouterments peculiar to range men riding a long trail.

The moon lifted. It soared high, casting a silvery sheen down the concave southern rampart of naked Ute Peak. It limned the stiff-topped pines and molded faint shadows upon the grass as Miggs went along toward his cabin first, and later, after shucking his pack and rifle, on over to the cow camp, a hundred yards beyond the cabin.

Brian was there when Miggs came up and dropped down, cross-legged, with a tired grunt. He had walked right along. Since most of that south-to-north trail had been uphill, and he had hurried, there was a good tired kind of weariness on him now.

The snub-nosed rider handed over a tin cup of steaming coffee. His friend, Lex Murphy, offered Miggs his tobacco sack and papers. Jack passed up the smoke but sipped that cow-camp coffee with relish. It put an edge to his hunger.

Fred Brian strolled over, cup in hand, looked down, and said: "You reckon it's too late to ride over and see this Holt feller this evening, Jack?"

It wasn't really late. The moon was up, the stars twinkled, but the sky was still powder blue. "By the time we got over where his camp is, Fred, it'd be right onto eleven clock. He's settled in over at the old Ute village grounds."

Brian puckered his brows, made a rough estimate, and said: "Three miles, Jack?"

Miggs kept watching the taller, younger man. Finally he put aside the tin cup, stood up, and said: "Come on.

It's going to make you fit and toss all night worrying about Holt's Durham bulls, so we might as well ride over right now and have it out, even if we have to roust them out of their bedrolls."

Miggs rode one of Brian's horses. The pair of them rode off with a handful of cooked meat from Red Morton's supper fire, passed on around the cabin bearing westerly until they came to the forest, then cut northward a little so as to strike a faint old trail Miggs knew that led directly to the old Indian campsite.

They didn't say much for the first mile, but, when they were well along into the second mile, Fred Brian suddenly spoke up.

"And if Holt won't move on westward," he asked. "What then, Jackson?"

Miggs looked over and looked back. The question had mildly surprised him. Always in the past Brian and Tolman had made their own decisions up here. He thought now he was being drawn into Hyatt Tolman's affairs deeper than he wished. He thought, too, of that letter in his pocket, and also of his assurance to Fred Brian that he would do what he could for Tolman's men and animals while they were in the uplands.

There seemed no honorable way out now, and to a man who had been a loner all his life, the prospect of being accountable to others was displeasing. Because he felt this way his answer to Fred was a little sharp, a little brusque.

"If he won't move westward, Fred, then I reckon either you'll have to move, your men'll have an awful lot of patrolling to do to keep his Durham bulls away from Tolman's grade Hereford cows, or we just live with it."

"That's no solution, Jackson. If he has more than four bulls, my riders and I won't be able to keep track of 'em, and even if we tried to, it'd never work."

Miggs said no more. His irritation increased as they rode along. Until today his biggest problem had been Jed Shafter's daughter. He'd had his doubts about how that other matter should be handled, but he'd been confident of ultimate success there. This, though, was very different. Aside from being placed squarely in between two bullishly stubborn cow outfits, his time, which had always been his own, now no longer was. He was obliged to aid Tolman's cattle and Tolman's range boss. It aggravated a loner no end to have claims made upon him against his will.

He did not, however, blame Fred Brian altogether. His judgment of Denver Holt after one meeting left him considering Holt and his men as something less than desirable neighbors. In fact, by the time they were within a half mile of the old Ute campground, a good deal of his private antagonism was directed against Holt just for coming into the uplands, instead of grazing his herds wherever he'd been grazing them the past years.

"I smell smoke," said Brian, sniffing the still night air.

Miggs nodded. He'd caught that scent farther back. He'd been watching through the trees for firelight. They were not very far, now, from the big grassy meadow with its bisecting white-water creek, which had once been the site of a large Ute village.

Through the forest's nighttime dark haze could be faintly seen a large, silvery meadow out beyond, where moonlight slanted downward, brightening everything. There was an occasional orange wisp of flame from a cooling campfire out there, and, just as they came to the last wooded tier of pines, loose horses became visible, meandering over the meadow, grazing.

Miggs drew up, dropped his reins, and sat a moment in formless shadows, studying that yonder cow camp. He had a feeling — he couldn't tell, though, whether this was a premonition of some kind, or simply the tag end of his earlier disgruntlement. Still, being a man whose life had hinged upon nothing more substantial than these little flashes at nerves' end many times before, he sat there sniffing the atmosphere, looking roundabout, trying to catch some inkling of what there was in this night that seemed roiled and unnatural.

Brian's face was a white blur as he watched Miggs and waited. Brian did not seem to catch any warning in the night at all. In fact, Brian seemed impatient to ride out into the clearing.

Jack stepped down, handed Brian his reins, and without a word went gliding to the last tree. There, he paused to look out, to rummage the meadow with his slitted eyes for some clue about that inner feeling he had.

He found it, too. A man with a carbine cradled in his arms standing guard southward a short distance, half in among the first fringe of trees, half out where moonlight limned him.

Miggs stepped back, fading out in the gloom. The Indians had been gone from these mountains for fifteen years. There were no animals up in here that would attack a man unless provoked. Then why the armed guard out so far from the main camp?

Perhaps, he thought, *because Holt felt it was the wise thing to do in a strange country.* No, Miggs told himself, *Denver Holt was a range man . . . he knew, after one sortie through a country, whether there could be any danger or not.* No, that wasn't it.

Miggs swung southward, passing wraith-like among trees until he was close enough to that unsuspecting cowboy almost to reach forth and touch him, which was his intention, but, in concentrating his entire attention upon that man, he'd neglected to sight another man coming through the trees, and this rider, having removed his spurs, made no sound at all over the pine-needle carpet.

The second cowboy saw Miggs, jumped behind a big tree, and let out a bellow of warning that galvanized the man he'd evidently come to relieve. Miggs reacted instinctively to that shouted alarm; he dropped flat.

Both those cowmen fired. Their bullets went whistling past Miggs. Over the echoes of those gunshot explosions other men's raised cries came on from the roused cow camp.

Miggs scuttled clear, whirled upright, dashed back where Fred Brian was standing beside their animals with his Winchester up and cocked, snarled for Brian to get back on his horse, and sprang upon his own mount.

They spun out, heading back the way they had come. Behind them crimson muzzle blasts erupted as Holt's entire force ran up and recklessly threw lead into the forest.

For a full mile Miggs and Brian sped along, narrowly missing being knocked off their animals a dozen times by low limbs and the irregular spacing of trees.

Jackson was in the lead; he knew this forest best. He halted after a while, calmed his agitated saddle animal, and swung his head as Fred came up. The pair of them exchanged a long look.

"That was my fault," growled Jackson Miggs. "I was watching the first one so close, I missed seeing the second one altogether."

But Brian brushed this aside. "That's not the point," he said angrily. "Why the devil didn't they sing out and give us a chance to identify ourselves? Hell, Jackson, if we hadn't lit out of there, they'd have killed us sure without even knowing who we were."

Miggs swung out and down, walked around his horse examining it, found no injuries, remounted, and sat with lips pursed and forehead deeply wrinkled for a while. He said nothing and apparently did not intend to say anything, so Fred spoke up.

"They'll likely have heard all that shooting back at our camp. We'd better head out, Jackson, before my boys decide to come up and investigate."

They started out again, still with Miggs leading. The last mile ended at the clearing opposite Brian's cow camp and Miggs's log house. At once both of them saw that Fred had been correct in his surmise. Both Lex

Murphy and Red Morton were rigging out their horses preparatory to mounting up.

Fred called to them, rode on up, dismounted, and began offsaddling. As he did this, he explained what had happened.

"We'll ride over in broad daylight," he announced, turning his animal loose. "Now, let's get some sleep."

Miggs finished caring for the animal he'd ridden and afterward turned without a word, heading for his cabin. Jackson Miggs was mad clear through.

Vagrant flickerings of Brian's campfire lit up the interior of Miggs's cabin. He glanced over to the partition where Beverly slept, put aside his rifle, and bent to kick off his boots.

Again that premonition brushed against his awareness. He straightened up very slowly, looking into all the corners of his cabin. Nothing moved, nothing seemed out of place. He swung for a closer look at Frank's bunk, walked over, and gazed upon the bulky coat lying atop McCoy's bed that he had mistaken for the outline of a sleeping man.

Miggs put up a hand, felt the coldness of McCoy's bed. Frank had not slept there in a long time. He went over to peer around Beverly's partition to see that her bed was also unoccupied.

Now he understood this second premonition. Neither Frank nor Jed Shafter's girl had come home from the downcountry camp. He stood a moment recalling Bev's prolonged absence. A chill ran down his spine. Something was wrong, bad wrong, or Frank would at least have returned.

Miggs took up his rifle, considered a moment, then put the gun aside for as long as it took him to exchange his boots for his moccasins, then he left the cabin soundlessly, skirted Fred Brian's cow camp where lumpy shapes lay, and broke into a steady jog, southbound through this ghostly, still, and empty night.

CHAPTER
EIGHT

Dawn was coming. Down the easterly slopes watery light shone in faint, blurred patches, but the deeper folds still retained night's gloominess when Miggs, cutting diagonally overland so as to approach his earlier campsite where he'd last seen Jed Shafter's daughter and Frank McCoy, came down a timbered watershed and halted upon a stingy little treeless promontory.

From this position he could see that precipice farther out that he and McCoy had stood upon the day before, watching Tolman's cattle approaching the uplands. Also from this site he could see that little clearing beside the still water pool where his camp with Frank and Beverly had been.

There was no sign of either the girl or Frank McCoy. It had been in his mind that he would find things as he now saw them to be. For that reason he had not taken the regular trail down, because then he'd have wasted an hour, perhaps more, picking up Frank's trail, and this way, satisfied that McCoy and the girl were nowhere near their former camp, he had only to descend into the cañon, which he did, and quarter back and forth between its nearly perpendicular granite walls, until he located the trail of a man wearing boots.

By the time the sunlight lay softly over the higher places of this tilted country, Miggs had the trail. He had determined from the idiosyncrasies of Frank McCoy, that this was in fact the trail he sought.

Evidently Frank, wearying of waiting for Beverly to appear, had gone in search of her. That much wasn't hard to deduce from the way McCoy's tracks stopped often, and the way he had grounded his rifle for the obvious purpose of freeing both hands so he could cup them to his mouth and call out.

The longer Miggs followed that trail the more concerned he became. He could also see that McCoy had been worried, too, for the tracks lengthened. McCoy, in making them had hurried along, obviously upset now as he approached a gentle rise that leveled out, which Miggs knew led up and over the northward bulwarks of this cañon he was in.

Climbing that easy, gradual lift from the cañon's depths, Miggs encountered warm sunlight near the plateau beyond. He also encountered something else. This second encounter left him feeling cold, fearful.

A mounted man had left his horse up here, tied to a straggly juniper tree. From the churned condition of the earth where that animal had stood, it had been tethered in this particular spot for at least one hour, perhaps even longer.

McCoy's boot tracks milled here. Miggs saw how Frank had kneeled — there was a knee-pad imprint — to test the shod horse imprints with a little twig, determining how long the horse had been there. He also saw the impression of Frank's rifle's steel concave butt plate, and his closely paced boot marks where McCoy had arisen to stand gazing northwesterly.

Now Miggs backtracked, a chilling notion in his mind. There had to be at least one more set of tracks where night gloom had hidden them from him before sunrise.

There were — not one set but two. The second set of tracks was small. Beverly Shafter's tracks! The second set, larger, high-heeled like a cowboy would make, showed also here and there little squiggles where spur rowels had raked along through deep dust and pine needles.

Miggs knew all he had to know for the moment. He returned to where the tethered horse had stood, picked up Frank's tracks again, hoisted his rifle, and broke over into that mile-eating Indian jog trot. There was a cold, deadly wrath burning in him as he jogged along. From time to time he glanced down, but he did not actually need McCoy's tracks any more, and neither did he need the clear imprints made by that shod horse — which was now carrying not just its cowboy, but Beverly Shafter, also, upon its back.

Time passed, heat came to loosen night-chilled muscles and sinews, spits of forest gave way to intermittent little parks, and with that big yellow disc approaching 11:00a.m., Jack Miggs skirted a brawling creek, leaped across it into a small grassy place, and heard a wild turkey gutturally call from off in the trees to the east. He halted, dropped to one knee, brought up his rifle, and hung there, waiting.

Frank McCoy stepped out into view.

72

Miggs stood up, brushed needles and dead grass from one knee, grounded his rifle, and waited, saying nothing at all by way of greeting as Frank came up, saying only: "Where is she?"

McCoy flagged vaguely northward. "I had a hell of a time of it. Too dark up until a couple, three hours ago, Jack. Mostly I went along following the stink of horse sweat to get this far."

"You haven't seen 'em?"

"In the dark? Of course not."

"It'll be one of Holt's men though, Frank."

"Yes."

"How long has he had her?"

McCoy leaned upon his gun. He had evidently given this some thought, for he said: "Probably since about noon yesterday. That's why she didn't come back to camp. Say since noon yesterday, and all last night, and up to now."

"Frank, I'm going to kill him. I don't give a damn who he is or what excuse he offers, I'm going to kill him."

McCoy looked quickly away from the white, wild expression of Jackson Miggs's face. He took up his gun, gazed off northward, and said: "Late last night I thought I heard gunfire far off to the north, Jack. Maybe someone else killed him for you."

Miggs hefted his rifle, too. He turned, set course, and started onward, saying over his shoulder: "No. That was Holt's crew opening up on Fred Brian and me."

"Huh? What'd you say?"

"Come along. I'll tell you while we're moving."

They passed back into the forest again, Miggs squirting out brittle, hard sentences until he'd told McCoy all there was to say. Then he abruptly stopped, turned, and glared.

"That's it! Frank, that's it. Fred and I couldn't figure out why they were all on edge like that last night. They didn't give any notice at all, just opened up like it was a war. They had her, Frank!"

McCoy, with no knowledge of how it had been the night before at Holt's camp, thought about what Miggs had deduced without seeming to believe or disbelieve.

"Let's get along," he said quietly, and moved out once again.

But Miggs's mind was moving now at top speed, his thoughts brittle cold and exact. "No, wait!" he called after McCoy. "Frank, you head for my place. Tell Fred and his riders what's happened. Bring them back with you to the old Ute village meadow. Fred knows the place. Bring them back with their guns and plenty of ammunition."

"What can you do alone?" protested McCoy, gazing uncertainly at Miggs's completely changed face. "Listen to me, Jack, if they was all nettled last night, think how they'll be this morning . . . an' you all alone sneaking up around their camp. They'll kill you sure."

Miggs would not listen. He made an imperative arm gesture, saying: "Go on, Frank. Trot all the way. Don't worry about me. There's no damned cowman living who can see me, if I don't want to be seen. Go on now."

74

Frank went, but not willingly. When he halted several hundred feet farther east and looked back, Jackson Miggs had disappeared.

The largest meadows below Ute Peak lay like a kind of irregular chain running roughly from southeast to northwest. In some places the strips of forest between those grassy parks were no more than three or four hundred feet wide. In other places they were nearly a mile wide. In those latter strips a kind of eternal gloom lay, rarely penetrated by sunlight because of the density of the trees. In these places Miggs made good time, trotting along Indian-like, whipping from place to place. But where the trees were thinner, the sunlight able to penetrate, he went much slower.

He was certain that fierce old Denver Holt would be more wary by day than he'd showed he was by night.

Twice, Miggs encountered bands of Durham cattle. Once he thought he heard a horseman passing along toward the largest of those uplands meadows, where the Holt cow camp was located, but it turned out to be several elk, cat-footing it charily westerly, and not a rider at all.

Then, closing in upon the brilliantly sunlit meadow with its tumbling, white-water creek, Miggs heard a horse nicker beyond the trees, and a second horse answer from within the forest, northward. He instantly faded out in a scrub thicket, peering upcountry. This time there was no mistake about it, a rider was moving quietly forward. He did not catch sight of that man until it was too late to intercept him.

When the cowboy passed from forest gloom into meadow sunshine, Miggs recognized him. It was that large, fearless-looking man who had lazily grinned when the three Holt riders had been caught, flat-footed, by Miggs and Frank McCoy at their first meeting. If he'd heard that man's name, he could not now recall it, but he did remember how that one had told the youngest cowboy to shut up. He also recalled the questions that older man had asked.

He felt cheated now, seeing that horseman ride out into full view of his friends farther across the big meadow. If he'd been able to catch that one and disarm him the second time, he felt sure he'd have learned the facts about Beverly Shafter's abduction.

When it was safe to do so, Miggs glided forth to the very meadow's edge, found another brush clump, and concealed himself in it, Indian-like.

They were breaking camp, out there. One man was packing the led horses, another was saddling and bridling. Denver Holt, recognizable as much by the arm he wore in a sling now, as by his oversize great bulk, waited slightly apart for the mounted man to come up, and afterward those two spoke briefly back and forth, then Holt crossed over where a big chestnut horse stood ground-hitched, snapped up the reins, and stepped up over leather. When Holt spoke to the man still working upon the ground, Miggs heard every word as clearly as though each one had been addressed to him.

"Curly says he found the cabin an' there's some cowboys camped there. He also says he run across a lot of driftin' white-face cross cattle. Them riders he seen must've just come up in here and brought those red-backs with 'em."

One of the dismounted men turned to gaze up. Miggs could not quite make out this man's face, but he recognized the similarity in build between Denver Holt and that man. It was Bert, Denver Holt's big, rough-looking son.

Bert said: "No one movin' down there?"

Denver didn't answer; the other mounted man, the cowboy Denver had called Curly, answered instead. "They were eatin' breakfast. There was three of 'em. They was camped downcreek a little distance from a log house, which I figure must belong to that burly-built feller who got the drop on us, and his string-bean pardner."

"Never mind all this talk," growled old Denver Holt. "Shake a leg. The cattle're driftin' north and west. We want to keep even with 'em."

Miggs hefted his rifle, gauged the distance, and estimated that he could knock Denver Holt out of his saddle without any difficulty, reload, and perhaps get one more of them before the others either rushed him or fled off into the westerly trees. He was calculating his chances when the cowboy called Curly spoke again, this time saying something that stopped Miggs's gun arm in mid-motion.

"I made a sashay south and around, comin' on back up here after I spied out those fellers, and ran across some tracks. Two fellers on foot, one of 'em, wearin' Indian slippers, was trailin' a mounted man. I lost the two on foot in the trees, but that other feller, the one on horseback, came right up to the very edge of this meadow, westerly there."

Miggs saw Holt, Holt's son, and those other two men turn and gaze at Curly. It was the son who finally spoke, saying: "What're you gettin' at, Curly?"

Curly shrugged. "I don't know. I just told you what I saw. Maybe it was one of those riders down there with the squawmen. Maybe it was a stranger passin' through."

The two dismounted riders looked away, went after their saddled horses, and paid no more attention to the Holts or to Curly.

Miggs, too, was puzzled. If that man he and Frank had trailed up here *had* been a stranger, one of the renegades who occasionally showed up in the remote Ute Peak country, then those yonder men were in the clear. He squatted in his place of concealment, turning this over in his mind, at the same time watching those horsemen across the meadow mount up, mill for a moment, then strike out westerly across the meadow toward the forest ahead.

It did not cross his mind until Denver Holt and his men were nearly lost to sight, that whoever that nighttime rider had been, he did not have to be a newcomer; it could've been any one of those five horsemen who had gone exploring and returned while the others were in their blankets last night. Could have returned in plenty of time with Beverly — or without her, in fact — to have still participated in that savage attack upon Fred Brian and Miggs.

Miggs stood up, leaned upon his rifle, and somberly watched the last of Denver Holt's crew disappear. Beverly had not been with them. That bothered him, too. Ultimately he decided the only way to ascertain whether or not one of those men had been the abductor was to talk to all of them. But more immediately important was to find Jed Shafter's girl. He was calm enough now, to think like this. Calm enough to consider first things first.

CHAPTER
NINE

Frank McCoy came along astride one of Fred Brian's pack horses, his long-barreled rifle balancing across his legs. He led the others out into the large meadow and on across to where Jackson Miggs was scouting the abandoned camp of Denver Holt's men.

There, they all dismounted, fanned out, and went over the ground a foot at a time. It was after midday when they came together again at the site of Holt's stone-ringed cooking spot.

"Nothing," grunted Frank to the others. "Jack, are you plumb certain she wasn't with them?"

Miggs nodded, looking withdrawn and deeply thoughtful. "She wasn't, boys, and that leaves only one thing to do . . . find her. Find her before we go after those others."

Fred Brian said: "That's your department, Jackson. I couldn't track a buffalo through a snowbank."

Miggs nodded. "Ride on westerly," he told Brian. "Don't let them see that they're being trailed, but find out where their new camp is. Then head back to the cabin. Frank and I'll meet you there."

"Sure," murmured Brian. "Good luck. Say, do you two need horses?"

Miggs shook his head, cradled his rifle, and jerked his head at Frank. The two turned away with no additional talk, went back to the western tree fringe where they'd abandoned the shod horse tracks hours before, and quartered for them again.

"Here," grunted Frank, the first to pick up those tracks. Then Frank straightened up, looked out where Brian and the others still stood, and strongly scowled. "Jack, it *had* to be one of them. Look there. He rode on out of the trees straight as an arrow for their camp. He probably offsaddled in the dark, slipped up, and got into his sougans without the others even noticing."

Miggs crouched over, stepped along to where that horse had left the forest for the meadow, paused there still crouched, then retraced his steps back to McCoy but did not stop.

"Come on," he muttered. "We've got about four hours of daylight left to backtrack him. He didn't take her into the camp with him, so he left her somewhere down his back trail and we've got to find that spot before sundown."

They went along slowly but steadily, at times being forced to halt altogether where the mounted man had crossed patches of weathered stone or brittle lengths of bone-dry pine needles. It was an exacting chore but for Jackson Miggs, a lifelong woodsman, it was never an impossible trail to follow, only an agonizingly slow one.

They ultimately came near the little glen where they'd met earlier when Miggs had been trotting along upcountry, and here Jack flung back an arm to Frank.

McCoy dutifully remained back where he was watching Jack quarter. When he thought Miggs should have all that sign read, he called ahead.

"What is it?"

Instead of answering Jack simply beckoned McCoy forward and struck off on an entirely new tangent. Now they were heading almost due east. But now, also, the trailing became much more difficult.

"It's her all right," said Miggs after a while, sounding pleased, sounding enormously relieved. "Right now I wish she weighed more so the tracks would be easier to see but at least, Frank, if she's walking along, she's alive."

McCoy made no comment for a long time. Not until they'd passed in and out of several forest strips. Then he said: "Jack, hold up a minute. The way we're going and have been going, is straight for your cabin."

"I know," retorted Miggs. "But if we hadn't been in such an all-fired hurry this morning, we wouldn't have missed the place where she either got away or he threw her off his horse. So let's keep on tracking this time, and, if she crawls into the underbrush or something, we won't rush on by."

"You do that," retorted Frank. "I'm going on ahead. I know that little lady . . . she's tougher'n a rawhide boot. She'll be at the cabin by now."

Miggs watched McCoy rush on easterly until Frank disappeared in among the trees, then he shrugged and continued his painstaking trailing of Beverly Shafter's sturdy, small tracks. He privately thought Frank was entirely correct, but, as he'd said, they'd hurried too fast once and missed finding the place where Jed

Shafter's girl and her abductor had parted company, and he did not want to risk losing her again.

He did increase his pace, though, where he dared do this, and once he neglected to seek the exact spot where the girl had crossed a fiercely tumbling creek and instead quartered the far side, picked up her sign, and went along it again.

He was still a goodly distance from his own meadow and his cabin when he heard a gunshot. He whipped fully upright and stood stockstill until a second shot came. That, he knew, was a signal, and since to his knowledge the only person still ahead was Frank McCoy, it had to be that Frank had found something.

Miggs hefted his rifle in the middle, held it down at arm's length, and broke over into that distance-consuming trot of his.

He had placed the exact spot that shot had come from. There was a little glade no more than two acres in size dead ahead. He made for this place, broke over into it out of the forest, and saw two things simultaneously. One, the most foremost object in his immediate sight, was a big, red-eyed bull elk with an enormously swollen neck from the rutting urge. The second thing he saw was Frank.

McCoy had somehow been separated from his rifle. The ferocious bull elk was pawing up big clods between Frank and his gun, which lay several hundred feet behind the red-eyed, frothing bull.

"Get down and stay down!" Miggs yelled. He had to move well to the north to be sure that no deflected bullet would strike anywhere near McCoy.

At his shout, though, that bull elk, easily fifteen hands high and weighing well over a thousand pounds, whirled and set himself to charge. He was, Jack could see plainly, insane with rage. There was no more deadly animal alive than these huge bulls who had gone out of their heads when the mating urge was on them. They would charge one man or a hundred men, completely blinded to the certainty of their own death. That was what this one did now — set himself for the charge.

Miggs stepped up beside a red-barked old fir tree, cocked his rifle, dropped to one knee, and aimed. He had only seconds to get set before that beast began his blind run. He caught that monstrous head over his sights, drew it down the barrel to him, and fired.

The huge bull seemed to freeze, to turn suddenly to stone. It was as though he was dumbfounded by the blast of that long-barreled rifle. He began to weave gently from side to side. A burst of gushing claret abruptly poured from his nostrils and with an earth-shaking crash he fell.

Jack stayed back until he'd reloaded, then stepped forth into plain sight. Frank McCoy, also, moved out into the little glade. He went over, retrieved his rifle, examined it carefully, then passed dourly over where Jack was coming to a halt beside the big bull elk.

"Good shot," said McCoy roughly.

"How'd he separate you from your gun, Frank?"

"I'll show you," muttered McCoy, turning to go back into the underbrush. Miggs followed. Where Frank halted, Miggs also stopped. He was gazing down at some crushed and broken underbrush. He stepped around Frank, kneeled, put out one finger, and trailed it across some bruised leaves.

"Blood," he said.

McCoy nodded. "Pretty fresh, too."

"Hers, Frank?"

McCoy nodded again. "It's got to be. There are no other tracks."

Miggs stood up, twisted to consider the dead bull elk, hoisted his gun, and jerked his head. "Go on like you were doing," he directed McCoy. "Head for the cabin. I'll continue tracking her out."

They parted again, Frank ignoring all but the most obvious sign, while Jackson Miggs passed along eastward at a much slower gait, picking up Beverly Shafter's tracks and carefully following and reading them.

After her encounter with the bull elk Beverly's tracks seemed much less positive than they'd been before. They paused often, and once, at a little seepage spring, the girl had obviously washed and rested before going on.

She was hurt, Miggs knew that, but he was heartened by the very fact that she could still walk along. In a way he blamed himself for what had happened to her. He should have given her a pistol, should have insisted that she wear one. But calm logic told him that, if she'd shot that bull elk, only wounding it instead of killing it, the big animal would certainly have killed her.

The same thing might even have applied to the man who had abducted her. If she'd tried to shoot whichever of the Denver Holt's men had stumbled upon her while crevice mining, he just might have shot back. It was possible that a man who would steal a girl would also kill one.

Less than a mile from the cabin the tracks of Jed Shafter's daughter began to straighten up again, to grow firm and steady in their onward striding. Jack Miggs sighed with relief. Whatever had happened between her and the cowboy, or between her and the bull elk, must not have caused her any bad hurt.

He came within sight of the cabin, finally, and paused a moment to look ahead. There was a little wispy stringer of wood smoke standing straight up into the golden daylight from his mud-wattle chimney. He saw no one, but then he probably wouldn't have anyway because his approach was from the cabin's rear.

One of Frank McCoy's horses nickered at the sight of him from up the box cañon. He looked up and looked back, stepped forth into his own clearing, and walked down to the cabin, and around it. The door was partially open so he eased through.

Frank was at the cook stove. Beverly had her back to the door.

Miggs said: "How are you, little lady?" And when she whipped around, the breath log jammed in Miggs's throat.

There was a bloody bandage on Beverly Shafter's upper arm and high on her right cheek was a purple bruise the swelling of which made her face lop-sided. Her normally good color was gone and in its place were dark rings around the eyes and a gray pallor elsewhere.

She made a ghastly little smile at Miggs and said: "I'm not as bad as I look. Frank told me how you killed that big elk. I walked right into him. He was browsing just across the clearing. I guess he didn't see me, either, but, when I walked near him, he made a noise like a trumpeter, and charged. I tried to get behind a tree but he knocked me down once before I got there. Afterward, I'm not quite sure what happened. I think I crawled behind the tree, but I'd bumped my head and things were foggy. I do remember crawling carefully away, though, keeping that big tree between us."

Miggs leaned his rifle upon the wall, strode over, and bent to examine her wounds closely.

McCoy spoke up next, saying: "He hooked her arm but aside from that, and the bump on her face, I think she's all right."

Miggs finished his rough examination, straightened up, looked grim as death, and said: "Which one of Holt's men took you out of that cañon where you were crevice mining?"

Beverly went to a bench, sank down, and shook her head at Miggs. "I didn't see him."

Miggs's eyes widened. "What? You were with him all last night and . . ."

"Jack," broke in McCoy quietly, "she was unconscious. He knocked her over the head with his pistol barrel. She's already told me that part of it." Frank went over to the girl, smiled, and said: "Bev, you climb into your blankets and rest. When that there gruel I'm making on the stove is ready, I'll waken you." He gave her an assist up off the bench and went with her as far as the little partition beyond which was her cot.

Miggs was still standing by the stove when Frank came over, jerked his head toward the door, and moved on across the room toward the outside sunshine and warmth. Miggs followed.

When they were out front, McCoy said: "She caught only one quick glimpse of him, Jack, and that was when his spurs made noise just before he came up behind her. She told me she turned to run . . . and that's all she remembers until she came to all alone by a little moonlighted meadow where he'd evidently dropped her thinking he'd hit her too hard and she was dead."

"That would be the meadow where we found her tracks heading for home," mused Miggs. "Frank, that one glimpse she had . . . was he big or short, thin or fat, young or . . . ?"

"He was just a silhouette in the trees and rocks to her. All she recollects is that he had spurs on . . . because she heard 'em."

Miggs went to a rough bench in front of his cabin and dropped down upon it. "We'll find out which one did it. If he had spurs that narrows the field, Frank. It was Holt or one of his men. We know that for sure now."

McCoy squinted at the reddening afternoon sun. "We knew that before," he calmly said. "Jack, I never in my born days saw as tough a woman as Bev Shafter is. No bigger'n a mite, but she took a gun barrel over the skull, a face to face run-in with a rutting bull elk, walked alone with blood running out of her arm near two miles, and, by God, when I walked into this cabin you know what she was doing? Fixing to cook supper so's we wouldn't have to go hungry when we came home."

Miggs solemnly nodded his head without speaking for a time. Everything within his sight was calm now and peaceful. He hadn't had much rest lately and he wasn't as young as he'd once been. Weariness welled up in him along with relief. She was safe. Bruised and hurt, but safe. He felt as a father would have felt, shaky and weak but tremendously thankful, too.

CHAPTER
TEN

It was after sundown when Fred Brian, Lex Murphy, and Red Morton returned to Miggs's clearing, put up their animals, and walked over to the cabin.

Jack and Frank were eating mush. They'd heard the cowmen ride up, but, knowing who they were, neither of them had gone outside to verify this. They were both dog-tired, whisker-stubbled, and edgy.

When Fred Brian knocked, Miggs called for him to enter.

The three riders came in out of the deepening dusk, Brian foremost. He looked from McCoy to Miggs and back to Miggs again.

"You find her?" he succinctly asked.

Miggs looked up, and saw the eyes of those three cowboys steadily widen, looking past him. Miggs turned.

Beverly was standing in the doorway of the space that had been partitioned off for her. She had washed and combed her hair. In the yellow lamp glow inside Miggs's cabin even the bruise on her cheek and the bandage on her arm could not entirely obscure the fact that she was very pretty.

She was staring, round-eyed, over at big Fred Brian. Miggs felt something like an electric shock pass back and forth between those two. He looked at Frank.

McCoy looked straight back at him, then Frank introduced Beverly Shafter to Hyatt Tolman's range boss and his two youthful cowboys.

Murphy and Morton swept off their hats with gallant flourishes, but Fred Brian stood there like a man suddenly struck dumb.

Beverly smiled a little self-consciously, crossed to the stove, and said, without looking back at any of them: "Maybe Mister Brian and his friends would like something to eat."

That broke the electrified atmosphere. McCoy got hastily upright, saying: "Sure, Bev, sure. Here, boys, sit down at the table. I'll fetch you some bowls of right fine gruel."

Jackson Miggs sat plumbing the depths of the confused and confusing atmosphere, gazing from Fred Brian to Beverly and on over at Murphy and Morton. It had not occurred to him that the girl's presence would make any difference. In fact he hadn't thought that far ahead at all, but he now realized that he should have. Three healthy young bucks, sturdy and in their prime, and a beautiful girl.

Brian sat down; so did his riders. Frank brought them bowls of mush and Beverly brought over three more tin cups and the coffee pot. She smiled at Lex and Red but did not look directly at Fred, only poured his coffee with her face profiled to Brian, wearing the faintest of approving looks, which, in the now comprehending view of Jackson Miggs, was almost a declaration of solid interest. Jackson, a lifelong reader of signs, read the faces of those two across the table from him with no difficulty at all.

He suddenly was no longer hungry or tired. The others talked, bantered Beverly a little, and questioned her about the man who had abducted her. Jackson heard all this but only indifferently; he was absorbed in something altogether new to him. He was looking at Fred Brian from the standpoint of a father, was measuring Fred's worth, dissecting what he knew of his disposition, his past, his future prospects, and it was all very disturbing to him.

Finally, when Frank sat back down, stuffed his little pipe and lit up, Jack caught his eye and jerked his head. McCoy calmly nodded and arose. The pair of them left the cabin scarcely noticed.

Outside, night was fully down and a strong rash of stars lay scattered across the high curve of heaven. Jack went over to a pair of small salt sacks Tolman's men had brought up with them for salting the cattle, eased down upon those sacks, and looked worriedly up at McCoy.

"It's one thing after another," he muttered. "We got her back alive . . . and now this."

Frank gazed down, puffed a moment, then quietly said: "This? What's *this*, Jack?"

"You know dog-gone' well what I'm talking about. You saw how he looked at her, Frank."

"Well, yes. And I also saw how she looked at him." McCoy removed his pipe, peered into its bowl, tamped the ashes with a thick thumb pad, raised his sly gaze, and considered his old friend.

"A lot goes on in the world a feller hardly ever comes across when he lives alone and apart, Jack. She's a good girl . . . clean and strong and sound as new money in limb and wind. He couldn't do better."

"I wasn't thinking of him, dammit."

"All right, let's reverse it. He's a big strong young buck. He's not a brawler or a drunk. He don't steal cattle or horses . . . so far as I know, anyway. He's got a good job with Hyatt Tolman. She could do a heap worse without half trying."

"Frank, you said yourself she's only eighteen or nineteen. Why, she's just a . . ."

"*Whoa*, old friend. Those pretty little Ute squaws used to get hitched when they was fifteen and sixteen. I've known my share of settlement girls that've done the same thing. Eighteen or nineteen is downright old for a gal to be getting married nowadays, Jack. Anyway, it's sort of with girls like it is with colts . . . if they're big enough, they're old enough."

Miggs picked up a little stick, examined it with a scowl, and turned it over and over in his hands. He was quite unused to the mood that was now upon him. In fact, he'd never before experienced anything like it. He was a simple, forthright man. Where civilization had complicated the lives and thinking processes of other men, it had never done this to him for the elemental reason that he'd made it a practice to avoid civilization.

Frank McCoy stood there hipshot, puffing his little pipe, fathoming to a surprising degree the mood and turmoil that plagued his old friend. In Frank's experience the things in life that tore at the heart and guts of men were seldom the things that had a price tag on them. They were instead, as in this case, events that involved a man's emotions, his beliefs, and his lifelong convictions, and he told himself, knocking dottle from his pipe, they were also things of which strong men were often quite ignorant.

Love, for instance, was something Jackson Miggs had never experienced. Not the love of a man for a woman or a woman for a man. Because it was foreign to him, he sat there now, torn apart by his doubts and fears, and, like most people with powerful doubts, he didn't want it to happen, didn't want it to intrude in surroundings with which he was thoroughly familiar and at home, because he was entirely ignorant of it. It frightened him.

"Frank?"

"Yes."

"Maybe I'm reading signs where none really exists."

"Maybe, Jack, maybe."

Miggs lifted his shaggy head, found Frank's eyes, and looked deeply into them. "You don't think so though, do you?"

McCoy pocketed his pipe and gently shrugged. "I've lived just long enough to know that where females are concerned, it does no good to try and second guess 'em."

"So we wait and see what develops. Is that it?"

Frank went over closer and squatted down with both long, skinny arms dangling off his bent knees. "Jack, if it happens, you can't stop it. Neither can I. Even old Ute Peak up there couldn't stop it. I've seen this happen before and one thing always stuck in my mind. There's no power on earth can turn back the attraction of a young buck or a young girl when the signs are right. And the man who tries is bound to find that out the hard way. I know how you feel, Jack. Hell, I'll even admit now that's why I brought her up here. I counted on you feeling that way. Not just because she was Jedediah Shafter's girl, but because I know you, Jack. You always have to help the weak and the lonely. You've been that way for twenty years. I was counting on you sort of fathering this little lady. But I sure never figured this other thing'd crop up, and that's a plumb damned fact. But it *has* cropped up, so now I've got to step in because I've seen a lot more of this than you have. Jack, you take my word for it . . . neither of us can stop it . . . and I'm not sure either of us has any right to try and stop it."

"But she's already been bad hurt up here, Frank. Damned if I'll stand by and see that happen to her again. Damned if I will!"

"What makes you think she'll *get* hurt? Listen to me . . . she's tough like her paw was. She's resourceful, too. You saw that today, the way she got clear of that bull elk and got back to the cabin, alone, through country she didn't know at all." McCoy shook his head from side to side with strong emphasis. "As for young Brian . . . you know him better'n I do, but I'm a fair judge of men and I say he's not the kind that'd hurt her."

"Maybe not," muttered Miggs, tossing aside the little stick he'd been holding. "Damn it all . . . I wish I knew, Frank. I wish I knew what lies ahead."

McCoy snorted, stood up, and gingerly kicked the stiffness out of his legs. "Don't we all," he said sardonically. "Don't we all. Come on, now, let's head back. I could go for one more cup of java before I turn in."

They were both standing erect preparatory to moving toward the house when two slim shadows passed across their view going out into the quiet night from the direction of Miggs's cabin.

Just for a second both these older men thought they were Brian and his men heading back for their camp, but because there were only two instead of three, and also because one was a good head shorter than the other, they stood motionlessly watching.

"Bev and young Brian," breathed Frank. He swung, looked gaugingly at Miggs, and said further: "Mighty nice night for a stroll."

Miggs said: "She ought to be in bed, her with a hurt arm and all."

McCoy made a wry smile into the darkness. "She's not even feeling that arm. Come on, let's get that coffee."

Miggs went, but he kept swiveling his head to gaze concernedly down where those two strollers had been. At the cabin door McCoy halted, caught Miggs looking worriedly back, and exasperatedly wagged his head.

"I sure overplayed my hand this time," he growled.

Miggs swung, faintly scowling. "What's that mean, Frank?" he demanded.

"Well, I knew you'd take to her. I knew you'd be good for her. But this acting like an old she-bear with just one cub . . ." McCoy shook his head again, pushed the door open, and stepped into the warmly lighted log house where Lex Murphy and Red Morton were soberly sitting, playing twenty-one at Miggs's big table.

Both cowboys looked up and around. Red said: "Miss Shafter an' Fred went for a walk. She figured it might not be a bad thing for someone to make sure the horses were all right."

"*She* figured!" exclaimed Jackson Miggs, scowling.

Red nodded. "Yup, she asked Fred to go with her."

Frank McCoy went over, dropped down at the table with a hard little knowing smile, did not look back at Miggs, and said: "Deal me a hand." He then swung toward Miggs. "How about that coffee, Jack? I expect these boys could use some, too."

Jack passed around the table to the wood stove, hefted the pot, shook it, found there was still plenty of liquid in it, poked up the coals, and set the pot over an open burner. He took four cups down from where Beverly had hung them after doing the supper dishes, placed them thoughtfully side-by-side and continued to stand there with his back to the card players, hearing their careless words and thinking of something entirely different.

When he eventually brought over the steaming brew Frank was ahead in the card game and, if any of those players, McCoy included, had anything besides the game on their minds, it neither showed in their talk nor in their expressions.

But Miggs had a desire to go back outside. He was in fact turning away from the table when McCoy's tired, rough voice reached out and halted him.

"Sit in for a few hands, Jack. I've always wanted to get a crack at some of that dang' money you've got cached away."

The two exchanged a long, knowing look. Miggs made no move back toward the table so Frank spoke again, this time selecting his words carefully so that their meaning was lost on Murphy and Morton but not upon Jackson Miggs.

"We'll get to Holt tomorrow . . . and everyone else who's out to hurt folks. But right now . . . that night out there is big and it's private. Especially private."

Frank looked over at Lex Murphy, who was shuffling the cards, and carelessly said: "Deal Jackson a hand. We need new money in this game. Besides, it sort of bothers me winning cash off nice young lads like you two."

"I'll sure bet it does," ironically replied Murphy, putting a baleful, loser's look upon raffish Frank McCoy. "I think that's actually a tear there in the corner of your eye, McCoy."

Miggs went over and eased down. He accepted the cards dealt him, and Frank McCoy, after one final look, forgot Miggs to concentrate on winning another hand.

A little later Beverly silently entered the cabin. She smiled at those four lifted faces, drifted over to stand briefly behind Miggs where she put a small, broad, nut-brown hand affectionately upon his shoulder. A moment later she went around behind raffish old Frank McCoy and did the same thing. After that, she told Murphy and Morton good night and disappeared around behind her partition.

Jackson Miggs let his breath out in one long, soft sigh, and concentrated on playing twenty-one.

Fred Brian did not come back into the cabin. The card players scarcely thought of him except to take it for granted that he'd gone on to his own camp and bedded down.

CHAPTER
ELEVEN

It was 5:00 a.m. and not quite sunup yet, when Lex and Red came hiking up to the cabin. Miggs wasn't there; he was up the cañon, looking after the horses, but he saw them and called softly before they awakened McCoy and Beverly Shafter with their knocking.

They went to where Jack stood, waiting. While still fifty feet off, Red Morton said from a worried face: "Fred's gone."

Miggs looked blankly from one cowboy to the other. "Gone. What d'you mean gone?"

"He didn't bed down last night. When Lex and I left the cabin, we never thought to go an' look at his blanket roll. We just naturally figured he was sleepin'."

"But he wasn't," put in Lex Murphy. "And this morning we could see that his blankets hadn't been slept in at all."

Something triggered alarm in Jackson Miggs. He turned without another word, went hiking out where Tolman's animals were, and counted them. One horse was not there. He went over where the pack outfits and saddles were hanging and counted those, also.

Evidently this had not occurred to the pair of cowboys, for now Red Morton stepped over, flicked a dangling rope, and said: "Hell, yes, Lex, he's ridden off somewhere. This is where he hung his rig yesterday when we come on back from shaggin' that Holt outfit."

Whatever Murphy's comment might have been, he didn't get a chance to voice it.

Jackson Miggs said roughly: "Saddle up, boys. Saddle up an extra pair of horses for Frank and me. Be fast about it."

Miggs was already striding rapidly toward the cabin before Morton and Murphy completely understood. He entered the cabin, went over and shook McCoy awake, made a motion for Frank to be silent, and told McCoy about Fred Brian's disappearance.

Frank sat up, ran his tongue around the inside of his mouth, ran bent fingers through his awry hair, and fixed Miggs with a watery glare. "He hasn't been took off, too, has he? Why would Holt want a big . . . ?"

"Wake up," snapped Miggs, fighting to keep his voice low enough not to awaken Beverly behind her partition. "Of course no one took him, Frank. Shake the cobwebs out of your skull, will you? He's gone over to settle with Holt."

McCoy sat abruptly upright. "Alone, Jack?"

Miggs said impatiently: "Get dressed. Lex and Red are saddling up for the lot of us. Fetch your guns and hurry outside."

McCoy tumbled out of bed, reached for his trousers, which were across the back of a nearby chair, jumped into them, and groped around under the bunk for his boots.

Jack went back outside. He had his long-barreled rifle, his six-gun holstered to his hip, and his big knife. He needed nothing more and took nothing more.

Murphy and snub-nosed Red Morton passed along toward Miggs from their cow camp. They, too, had six-guns, but their other supporting weapons were the ubiquitous Winchester carbines of cattlemen. This gun, one of the best short-range guns of its kind, was almost indestructible, but it could not, within a hundred yards, compare with Miggs's and McCoy's long-barreled rifles for either range or cold accuracy. There was one consolation, though — Holt's men, being cowboys, too, would have no better guns.

Miggs stepped out to come alongside one of the led horses. He was mounting when the cabin door opened. Frank McCoy came out with a screwed-up face, flapping shirt tail, and his weapons, and stood there, blinking at a fresh new day, and let off a deep-down, growled curse.

The four of them slow-paced their way across Miggs's meadow to the yonder trees, swung westerly, and said nothing to one another for a half mile, after which Frank asked garrulously just where, exactly, they were going.

"It's about five miles from here," explained Red Morton, twisting to look back at McCoy. "There's a white-water creek an' meadow cut in two by a long erosion gully."

Miggs placed the site at once. It was, in fact, one of his favorite winter trapping places. Some thirty years earlier militiamen, chasing marauding Utes, had cornered a band of Indians in that gully and wiped them out to a man. There were still some rusted old guns down there, not to mention an assortment of bones that were not exclusively those of Ute war horses.

"Know the spot?" Frank asked Miggs.

"Yes, I know it."

"Then let's dust right along."

Miggs shook his head. "No need. Besides, we couldn't make much better time than we're making right now. And, Frank, to be on the safe side, we can't get hurt saving these horses."

"Sure, but . . ."

"Listen, Fred's been gone most of the night. Whatever he had in mind, he's probably already done. Killing ourselves and our animals won't reverse that."

McCoy subsided, riding along tucking in his shirt tail, muttering uncomplimentary epithets about being yanked out of a good sleep, and alternately cursing Fred Brian for a fool, and beseeching some vague deity to preserve Brian from whatever tomfoolery the range boss was up to.

The sun climbed steadily, warming them whenever they crossed over one of those upland parks. By the time they were within a mile of the place that Red had indicated was where he and Lex and Fred had trailed Denver Holt and his crew to their new cow camp, Jack was in the lead. Frank was directly behind him, and Brian's two cowboys were strung out behind McCoy.

Jack halted at a spring to get down, drink, and water his animal. When the others clustered around, Miggs said: "Red, we're going to leave these horses in a little while. You stay with 'em while the rest of us go on afoot and scout up Holt's camp. Whatever happens, don't let Holt set us afoot."

After they had all watered and rested, Miggs led them ahead, but from here on he cut and quartered, seeking Fred Brian's tracks. He found them less than a half mile from the forest's ending where Holt's camp was distantly visible in the large broken meadow dead ahead.

He also found something else. The exact spot where a second man had appeared, coming up from behind Brian on foot.

"And that," exclaimed Frank McCoy dryly, "is that!" He proceeded to point out to Morton and Murphy how one of those men had driven the other one on ahead of him out across the cow camp meadow.

"Brian's probably a real good cowman," allowed Frank, "but he hasn't a brain in his danged head when it comes to walking into traps with both eyes wide open."

Jack Miggs privately agreed with McCoy, but, instead of saying so, he dismounted, tossed his reins to Morton, crooked a finger at Frank and Lex, then started onward to the forest's final fringe of irregularly spaced big trees.

"If we knew what time they got Fred," Frank softly said to Miggs, "we'd know about what they might do next."

"Not much they can do," retorted Miggs, squinting over the big green meadow in dazzling sunlight. "He didn't shoot anyone or run off any bulls. I doubt like hell if he even got to ask any questions. Kind of hard, being orry-eyed and fired up to fight, when some feller's got his cussed six-gun zeroed in on your kidneys from the rear."

The cow camp of Denver Holt and his men was a long half mile on across the large meadow. It was, in fact, on the far side of the erosion arroyo that bisected the park. Perhaps if the sun had not been so dazzlingly bright and sharp, they could have made out more than they did, but at any rate it appeared to Jackson Miggs that Holt's camp was either empty of men, or else they were hiding, perhaps in that intervening deep arroyo.

"In some predicaments," Miggs said conversationally to Frank and Lex Murphy, "camping out in a big clearing like that is about the same as committing suicide. But in this case, it isn't."

"Yeah," grumbled McCoy, "how do we get over there without being seen for half a danged mile before we're even close? Old Holt played this one smart . . . he's about as far from the surrounding trees on any other side as he is from this spot right here."

Miggs looked up. "You want to ride out, Frank, with your hand, palm out, to show 'em we come in peace?"

McCoy glared. "You crazy, Jack?" he demanded. "Maybe with Utes a feller'd have at least half a chance. But with that Holt outfit . . . uhn-huh . . . they cut loose on us before without even singing out. I wouldn't ride out into plain sight, even of their empty camp. That's a rough, tough bunch of cattlemen, that bunch."

"Lex," said Miggs, "you got any ideas?"

"Fire the grass if it was dry, but, since it ain't dry, no, I got no ideas at all."

Miggs drew back, stood straight up, hooked both arms around his rifle, and gazed out for a long time before saying: "There's a way. It's not very good, maybe, but it's the only thing we can do. Frank, I'll ride out loose and easy. If anything happens, I'll duck down and side ride back here. If that happens, you two give me a lot of cover fire."

"Side ride?" called Lex Murphy, looking troubled.

McCoy said brusquely: "Hang one heel behind the cantle of your saddle, drop all the rest of yourself down out of sight over the side of your horse. If you got to shoot, you do it by firing under your horse's neck." McCoy finished his explanation, squinted at Miggs, and said: "How about singing out first?"

"No good, Frank. That way we wouldn't, even one of us, ever get close enough to see whether Brian's in their camp or not."

"Doesn't look to me like anyone's in it," commented Lex Murphy. "Still as midnight out there."

"Sure," growled Frank. "If a feller doesn't want anyone to know he's lying low, waiting for a good shot, he's not likely to run up a flag saying . . . 'Come on in, I'm waiting.' "

Murphy swung to put a swift, indignant stare upon McCoy, but he said no more and neither did Frank. Miggs, satisfied with what he'd seen, jerked his head at the other two and started back for the horses.

Red Morton stepped out in front of the animals, held up one hand for silence, and faced southward. At once the others also turned and halted.

For a long moment there was no sound at all. Jack caught Frank McCoy looking at him; he was on the verge of heading along for his horse when he heard it — the faraway sound of lowing cattle and shouting men.

Lex Murphy reached up, scratched the tip of his nose, puckered his brow, and said to Red Morton: "Those aren't our critters. The sound isn't right."

"Probably this Holt outfit's gatherin' up their cattle to push 'em somewhere else," responded Morton.

"I know a good way to find out," said Miggs, and went over, swung up, shortened his reins, and waited for the others to get astride. When they had, he said: "Frank, take 'em down through the trees and see what's happening. I'm going on out to their camp and look for sign."

McCoy looked first southward toward that oncoming noise, then westward where Miggs was riding down through the last tier of trees and out into plain sight upon the yonder meadow. Frank seemed uncertain. Neither he nor the two cowboys made any southward move for a long time, not until they saw Miggs cross half that big meadow without incident.

"All right," McCoy muttered then, "let's go see what Mister Holt's up to."

The three of them picked their way carefully toward the distressed bawling of driven cattle. They did not look back to see what had become of Miggs, and Jack did not look toward them, either, as he rode openly in the direction of the cow camp that he now knew was deserted for some reason, while Holt made a gather of his Durham cattle.

The camp itself was typical; trappings of the cowman's trade lay carelessly scattered. There was no one anywhere around, and even a careful examination of the big erosion gulch provided Miggs with nothing to go on in his search for some sign that Fred Brian had been here.

He did find something, though, which he appropriated and which brought up that earlier antagonism in him again for Denver Holt and his men. This object was a small, bloodstained handkerchief, the kind women and girls carried. He pocketed it, got back astride, listened a while to all that oncoming bawling, drifted southeasterly out of Holt's meadow and back into the forest, heading downcountry on the trail of his friends.

He could not at once imagine what had become of Fred Brian. But neither could he imagine any reason for Holt to be gathering his cattle. He had made it very plain that he would not move unless he felt like it.

Jack found McCoy, Murphy, and Morton down in a little skiff of second-growth firs, sitting their saddles, looking straight out where the first of a big bunch of Durham cattle were pushing on out into the open from a southerly stretch of gloomy forest. There was no rider leading these animals, but farther back, on both sides of the cattle, he and the others heard men hooting and catcalling, urging still more cattle northward.

Jack and Frank exchanged a bewildered look. Jack reached out, brushed Red Morton's rein hand, and said: "What would the reason be for gathering now?"

"No reason that I can see," retorted the younger man, and swung back to watching the increasing numbers of those big brown cattle break out of the southward forest.

CHAPTER
TWELVE

Denver Holt's cattle were streaming past on both sides of Jackson Miggs and his companions before a single rider appeared across the southern meadow.

The first cowboy was that fiery, younger man Miggs recognized from his first meeting with Holt's crew. The second one was Denver Holt himself, his broad-brimmed hat pulled low, his bearded face dusty and grim-looking. The final rider was that dark-eyed and curly-headed large man who'd grinned and kept on ironically grinning when Miggs and Frank McCoy had gotten the drop on him and the other two.

"Well," snub-nosed Red Morton said, drawing back to sit beside Miggs, "that's that. Now we'd better get out of here before they get up this far."

Morton was reining around, so was Lex Murphy, but sly Frank McCoy did not move except to swivel his head and put a wondering glance upon Miggs.

"One missing!" he exclaimed.

Miggs nodded, still watching those oncoming men. "So I noticed. And I think I've got this figured out, boys."

Miggs spun his horse without another word, led out back northward again, and, when the four of them were ahead of Holt's cattle, Jackson peeled off westerly, leading the others straight as an arrow for that exposed, sunlit cow camp.

Murphy and Morton exchanged an uncomfortable look about this. Although neither of them voiced it, both thought it was extremely rash to ride out into the exposed meadow when Holt and his crew were no more than twenty minutes behind them.

But Miggs was gambling that his suspicions were correct. As soon as he and Frank McCoy were close to the camp, Miggs made an encircling motion with one hand, Indian fashion, swept that same hand up toward his face with the first two fingers pointing at his eyes, then dropped the hand, pointing earthward and beyond. Frank, who understood *wibluta*, nodded and rode on around the camp to do as Miggs had told him in sign language: Go back and forth, watch the ground, pick up fresh horse tracks.

Frank hadn't ridden twenty feet westward before he raised an arm, whistled, and pointed downward. The others hurried over, saw the sign where two ridden horses had gone due west from Holt's cow camp, and began following that definite sign.

The foremost of those horse tracks had been made hours before, had in fact been made while there was yet dew on the grass. But the second set of tracks had been made much later, after the dew was gone, and they were therefore less indelibly printed and harder to follow.

When Frank complained about this, Jack Miggs shrugged. "We only need one set. Brian's after him.

Where one set goes, the other will also go." Miggs lifted his head, looked up into the forest that they were now approaching, and said: "I don't understand, if Brian was taken prisoner, over there, when he rode up last night, how he got loose to follow young Holt."

McCoy had a different notion. "I read it to be young Holt following Fred Brian. I'd guess Brian got loose before sunup . . . that'd account for the dew tracks . . . got a horse, and slipped out, then young Holt went after him come sunup after they discovered Fred was gone."

Miggs ran this through his mind, and ultimately accepted it, saying of his earlier idea: "I guess when a man's got just one thing on his mind, he bends the facts to fit his notions. You're right of course, Frank. Bert Holt is trailing Fred Brian."

"And if that's so," said McCoy, "then my guess is that Brian's unarmed and young Holt's got plenty of firepower. It might help if we sort of dusted it along."

As they entered the forest where it was not possible to make great speed, they nevertheless hastened as much as this business of reading tracks would permit. Once, when the four of them halted to water their animals, Jack Miggs explained an idea he'd been perfecting since they'd first picked up the tracks they were following.

"Holt's moving those cattle for a good reason. He figures that if Brian gets back to us with whatever he's learned about Beverly's abduction, we'll come a-gunning."

"That's likely enough," Red Morton agreed.

"So," went on Miggs, "he sent his boy to run Fred down and kill him if he can, while he and the balance of his crew rounded up the Durhams and headed them on out of the country."

"Makes sense," agreed McCoy.

They resumed their tracking, sometimes making good time when they crossed a meadow, sometimes being forced to go very slowly in among the trees. It was not yet midday when somewhere off in the distance to the left each of them heard the faint pop of a gunshot. They halted, awaiting a repetition, but no other shots came.

Now Lex Murphy said, with his face perplexedly twisted: "The danged tracks are heading west still. That shot came from south and east, below us and somewhere behind us."

"Maybe it was the old man or one of his riders," suggested Red Morton. "Maybe one of 'em was signalin' to the others . . . somethin' to do with the cattle."

"Yeah," growled Frank McCoy, his narrow face twisted in the direction of that gunshot. "And maybe it's young Holt and maybe he's run Fred Brian to earth and is trying to finish him."

Miggs said nothing until each of the others had his say. Miggs was more worried by that shot than perplexed by it. "We've got to split up," he announced. "I hate to do it this way, but, if Frank's right, then Fred needs help." He bobbed his head at Lex Murphy. "You go with Frank . . . the pair of you find out where that shot came from and why it was fired. Red, you stay with me. We'll go on tracking Holt and Brian, and, if the tracks bend around and start down in the direction of that gunshot, we'll meet Lex and Frank. If not, we'll keep going until we find . . . something."

None of them appeared enthusiastic about this plan, but, as they briefly sat there considering it, none of them could come up with a better alternative, so in the end they reluctantly split up and rode their separate ways.

Miggs and Red Morton sat still until Lex and Frank McCoy were lost to sight, southward bound through forest gloom and the depthless hush, then they returned to tracking. Because Miggs was anxious now, he sometimes made detours and short cuts, in this fashion attempting to shorten both the job he'd saddled himself with and the time involved in following out the sign of those two hurrying riders somewhere ahead.

An hour later, as he and Red were crossing another grassy glade, the tracks abruptly swung southward. Miggs thought, and told Red, that Brian had discovered that he was being pursued now. He pointed to a place where a rider had halted out in the meadow, turned his horse, and had sat a long moment, looking back.

"He heard something," Miggs conjectured. "He's coming to the conclusion that he's being chased."

Miggs reined his animal dutifully southward and began trailing on this new tangent. At his side Red Morton said: "Now we're headin' about right. If the tracks cut back eastward, we'll know Brian's ridin' for either our camp or your cabin."

Miggs muttered a comment on this without looking up from his study of the ground. "And we'll also know something else, Red. We'll know that gunshot wasn't anyone signaling someone else . . . unless it was young Holt trying to catch the attention of his friends so they'll head Fred off."

Red frowned, lifted his head, and swung it eastward. "Yeah," he growled, "Holt will likely have been close enough to maybe shoot Fred's horse, or something."

Miggs said no more.

They left the meadow, following the tracks down through the trees again, but, instead of bearing south, the tracks began now to veer more easterly. Miggs was convinced that shot had been young Holt firing at Brian. He also became convinced that unless Divine Providence interceded, Lex Murphy and Frank McCoy were going to ride straight into a hornet's nest, because, aside from Bert Holt, the rest of Denver Holt's crew and the old cowman himself, were somewhere southeastward, pushing their Durham cattle along.

But Miggs did not hurry. When Red spoke about this, Jack said: "Maybe an hour back, if we'd known which way to go, speed might have helped. But do a little figuring now, Red, and you'll realize we're getting almighty close to the place where someone fired that shot, and, also, we're not too far south or west of either Holt's camp or his cattle drive."

Morton subsided, but he still acted anxious. He rode along, paralleling Miggs for a while, then gradually increased the distance between them, staying well above the tracks Miggs was following, so as not to impede

115

Miggs's progress. In this way Morton got a long three hundred feet ahead. He was visible to Miggs only now and then as he passed from one shadowed, forested place to another.

In this manner the pair of them traveled a mile farther east before both were halted stock-still by a sudden outburst of furious gunfire seemingly not more than a thousand yards ahead.

Morton at once dropped back where Miggs was dismounting. "Bring your Winchester," said Miggs as he hid his horse in a pine thicket. "Hurry up!"

Morton moved fast but Miggs darted off among the trees, leaving the cowboy to catch up as best he could. They came together again, heading north by east, and if Red Morton had no very clear idea of distances or directions in the forest, moccasined old Jackson Miggs had enough woodland savvy for them both. He also knew this uplands country beneath Ute Peak better than anyone alive.

"About like I figured," he whispered to Morton as they glided along. "Frank and Lex ran into Holt's riders with the cattle. That shooting came from south of Holt's camp."

But except for that one fierce volley of gunfire the forest was utterly still again. There was not another sound until Miggs and Morton angled across the white-water creek that bisected Holt's meadow and ran southward down through the forest where they were sneaking along.

This second rash of shots, though, seemed uncertain. First, someone fired a six-gun. This blast came from off eastward. Next, someone cut loose with a rifle. This brought on another ragged volley, but when these shots dwindled, silence returned.

"Frank," said Miggs succinctly to Red Morton.

"That was a rifle, not a carbine, or a six-gun. It's Frank and he's west of us. Come on . . . we'll find him."

They switched course, recrossed the brawling white-water creek, went silently trotting in and out of rough-barked stands of giant trees until a sunlit broad expanse of grassland shone on ahead, then Miggs halted, looped both his massive arms about his rifle, and stood entirely still and watchful.

"That's Holt's meadow," he told Red Morton. "We rode in one hell of a big circle this morning."

"All right," assented the anxious range rider. "But where is McCoy? Where is Fred?"

"Easy," remonstrated the older man. "We'll find Frank. I can't even guess about your range boss, but we'll find Frank and Lex. Just be patient."

For a long time that savage silence ran on. Morton fidgeted, but Jackson Miggs, except for keeping a hawk-like look-out all around, remained motionless and passive.

Someone eastward let out a bellow and fired a gun. At once that rifle made its sharp, biting sound again.

Miggs smiled frostily, took up his gun, and jerked his head. "I've got the direction again," he said. "Come on."

Again they slipped through the forest shadows, but this time Miggs did not stop until, at the very fringe of

117

the meadow, he paused to gobble like a wild turkey. An answering gobble came back. Miggs headed straight for this sound. Red followed, and gave a tremendous jump when old Frank McCoy rose up from the ground almost directly under Morton's feet. Frank's grease-stained buckskin clothing matched the ground perfectly. He grinned at the startled cowboy, screwed up his face, and spat aside as Morton and Miggs dropped down beside him.

"I figured you'd pull a bonehead stunt like blundering right into them," said Miggs, sounding not at all disgusted, sounding instead as though this situation amused him.

"Blundered into 'em, hell!" exclaimed McCoy. "I did this on purpose."

"Sure you did," growled Miggs, straining ahead for sight of the hidden cowmen on around the meadow, also in among the trees.

"That's a fact," spoke up a new voice as Lex Murphy came up. "They got Fred. The old man's boy shot the horse plumb from under him and the others came up. We saw them get Fred when we got down here, too. Two of 'em wanted to kill Fred and hide the body. They argued about that for a long time, then Frank and me, we figured we'd better give 'em something else to worry about before the hold-outs got tired of arguin' and salted Fred down, so we opened up on 'em."

Miggs turned, put a wry glance upon Murphy, drifted this same gaze back down to Frank McCoy beside him, and said: "All right . . . you've had your say.

Now get your belly down on the ground before one of 'em blows your liver out."

Murphy dropped down. Red Morton went over beside him, also got down, ran a careful look ahead where a little skiff of dirty white smoke hung among the trees where Holt's crew was forted up, then swung to say to Lex: "I'll be damned if those two old devils aren't gettin' a big kick out of this. Look at 'em grin."

Murphy looked, saw Frank and Jackson Miggs kneeling side-by-side, both of them looking careful and interested and raffishly amused, and said to his pardner: "Red, the devil himself couldn't scare those two. By God, I'm glad they're on our side."

CHAPTER
THIRTEEN

For a long time there was no movement and no sound over where Denver Holt and his men lay prone in the shadows. Frank tried the old trick of hurling a stone to draw gunfire. It didn't work and Jack Miggs hadn't thought that it would.

"They're not greenhorns," he growled at McCoy. "But if you really want to draw some fire and get 'em moving, jump up where they can see you and holler."

"You," replied McCoy quietly, "can go plumb to hell."

"Be pretty lonesome down there with you up here," said Miggs, and inched forward where he could see better.

"That's right," McCoy said sarcastically, "play the hero and get a hole through your skull for the effort."

"I was getting sleepy back there," retorted Miggs in the same vein. "Tell you what, Frank, they've got Brian, so in the end it'll occur to them to call out for us to quit or they'll kill him, so I figure I'll slip around behind them if I can and catch us a hostage, too."

McCoy brushed pine needles from one arm and nodded. "All right," he agreed. "It might work, but watch out, Jack, that's a blamed rough crew over there."

Miggs was crawling off when Red Morton pushed frantically forward and hissed at him: "Jack, don't be a fool! They'll get you sure."

Miggs looked back, said nothing, looked ahead, and continued on his way.

"Stop him," Red ranted at Frank. "They're all fired up over there. They'll see him sure."

"Might smell him," opined Frank, lying relaxed, "but they'll never see him, boy. Just you get back down now and quit sweating."

Something moved within McCoy's yonder sight. In a twinkling he had his rifle snugged back. He fired, ducked down, and hastily wiggled clear of the place he'd fired from. At once a blast of gunfire came back, cutting low limbs and striking tree trunks with solid, ripping sounds.

Red Morton and Lex Murphy hugged the ground until this gun thunder subsided, then cautiously looked up.

Frank McCoy was no longer in sight.

"Damn it," breathed Red Morton, agitated, "those two fools have went and left us alone out here."

Murphy considered, rose up, and began crawling along after McCoy. Once he turned to jerk his head at Red, and Morton began scuttling southward deeper into the trees, also.

They came upon Frank, standing like stone beside a tree. McCoy wagged his head at them. "If you're coming with me," he grunted, "take off those damned spurs."

The three of them went along again when both riders had shed their spurs. Frank led and he was not only silent and wraith-like in his movements, he was also difficult to emulate because he moved in fits and starts, with long, listening, watching pauses in between.

After a while, though, McCoy jutted with his chin, saying only one very quiet word: "Yonder."

It took a while for the cowboys to see anything ahead at all, but they ultimately sighted blurred movement where Jack Miggs was closing in upon the place Holt's men were firing from. Their attention, though, was abruptly diverted by a sharp, alarmed curse from Frank McCoy.

The older man flicked his head meaning for both riders to duck out of sight. They both obeyed instantly, although neither of them saw any reason to do so, not at once anyway. Not until Frank faded out, too, crept up, and put his lips close to whisper: "Someone's coming this way behind Jack. Didn't either of 'em see the other."

"Who?" asked Lex Murphy, and old Frank made a face.

"How the hell do I know who? But we'll fix up a little welcoming committee for him, whoever he is. You two get over toward the meadow and behind separate trees. Don't do anything at all until I turkey gobble at you. Understand? Now go on."

Frank could no longer make out Jackson Miggs at all. He didn't make any great effort to do this, either, for that spurless cowman was getting closer now, and he seemed to be no novice at slipping quietly through a forest. His biggest mistake, in McCoy's view, was to bring along a shiny carbine. But it was not to be expected that this man would attempt to flank Frank and the others armed only with a six-gun.

Still, McCoy faintly and disapprovingly shook his head. Even the greenest buck Indian knew enough to wrap his gun in cloth or underbrush to keep sunlight from reflecting off it. Frank's respect for the oncoming enemy dropped steadily; it did no good to be quiet as an Indian if you also carried a mirror, which was about what this shiny carbine amounted to.

Morton and Murphy had faded out northward. Frank looked for them, satisfied they were both out of sight, and turned to consider ways of intercepting the oncoming man without shooting. As long as Jack Miggs was ahead somewhere, it would be best not to arouse Holt's men, if this possibly could be done.

The cowboy, while gliding from one tree to another, crossed a shaft of golden light. He turned his head and Frank recognized him as the hotheaded younger cowboy he'd met once before under unpleasant circumstances. Frank carefully leaned his rifle against a tree, got down flat, and wiggled into the thick, soft, and fragrant layers of underfoot pine needles. He remained like that, blending perfectly into the gloomy shadows until that cowboy came up, passing along northward, and eased silently on by. Frank lifted his six-gun, waited for the rider to move again, and, when the rider did, Frank did not say a thing — he simply cocked that six-gun.

The rider froze. He was between two trees, thoroughly exposed. That little metallic sound did its work precisely as Frank had expected it to. Holt's man was neither foolish enough to try outrunning a bullet, nor to whipping around and risking a snap shot, for, no matter how fast he was with a gun, he couldn't hope to draw and fire before McCoy dropped him.

Frank got up, slapped needles and crumbly earth off his clothing, walked over, and disarmed the cowboy. He didn't have to call for Morton and Murphy; they had seen the capture made and now slipped up to examine McCoy's red-faced and wrathful prisoner.

McCoy put up his gun, stepped around in front of the cowboy, and said: "What's your name, sonny?"

"Clark Forrester, you damned old . . ."

"Easy now, sonny, don't start abusing folks or you might get your skull busted like a ripe pumpkin."

"Not by you," snarled the cowboy. "Or anyone like you, you damned old reprobate."

Red Morton said not a word. He reached out, tapped the cowboy, and, when Clark Forrester turned, surprised to find that he and McCoy were not the only ones out here, Red swung. Forrester took that blow flush upon the point of the jaw and collapsed in a limp heap. Red blew on his knuckles and muttered something about bony-jawed men.

Frank looked down, looked up, and said dispassionately: "I expect one of us had to do that." He had scarcely finished speaking when a gun exploded on ahead. Without bothering to know anything more, all three of them dropped flat beside their unconscious prisoner.

There was no answering shot.

Frank looked at Murphy, then at Morton. "It'd be a shame," he said, "if Jack was to get shot trying to catch us a live one, when we've already got Mister Forrester, here. I'll tell you, boys, you both stay and keep Mister Forrester here from waking up and letting out a yell, and I'll go fetch Jack back."

McCoy didn't wait, but slipped off among the trees and disappeared almost at once from the sight of Red Morton and Lex Murphy.

He went steadily ahead toward the spot where he'd last seen Miggs. When he arrived in the vicinity of the place, he stood for a long time while keening the air, testing it as an old hunting dog might have done. There was no sign of Miggs but that meant nothing.

On ahead through the trees Frank heard men's voices in blurred, careful conversation. He got down low, passed still closer, and, when he stopped this time to peer out, a twig brushed lightly over his shin bone. He didn't jump, he simply turned his lowered head, met Jack Miggs's indignant stare, and jerked his head for Miggs to go back.

When the two of them were a hundred feet away and before Miggs could remonstrate with McCoy for coming up, Frank explained about Clark Forrester. Miggs was more surprised that the cowboy had gotten around behind him, than he was at the actual capture of Forrester.

He stood for a moment in quiet thought, then whispered: "All right. Get out of sight, Frank. I'm going to hail Holt and offer him Forrester for Fred Brian."

McCoy stepped behind a big tree. Miggs, moving over beside another large pine but staying out in sight, let off a bull-bass call. "Holt! Denver Holt!"

For a moment only the echoes of that outcry came back, then a voice equally as deep and powerful replied.

"What do you want?"

"This is Jackson Miggs, Holt. I've got a trade for you."

"What're you talkin' about, Miggs?"

"You've got Fred Brian, haven't you?"

There was another pause, then Holt yelled back: "We've got him . . . what about it?"

"We've got Clark Forrester. You turn Fred loose and we'll send Forrester back to you."

Holt did not reply at once to this. Miggs stepped back around his tree, looked over, saw Frank watching him, and looked back eastward again. It was no longer possible to hear voices over where Holt's men were, but it was not hard to figure out that a discussion was under way over there. After what seemed an agonizingly long period of time Denver Holt's roar came back.

"All right, Miggs! Send Forrester back and we'll turn Brian loose."

Jack jerked his head around at Frank. "Go back," he said, "and fetch that cowboy up here."

McCoy left in a rearward trot. Miggs called out, stating that he'd sent back for Forrester.

Holt accepted this, then called out again: "Miggs, you keep out of my way! I owe you something for wingin' me. This is no warnin', Miggs, this is a promise!"

Jack's face hardened against the arrogance and the bullying tone of that big voice. He called back, saying: "Sure, Holt, I'll stay out of your path . . . the second you hand over to me the man who hit Beverly Shafter over the head and rode off with her! When you do that, I'll be content to stay well clear of a skunk like you, for I never did like the smell of your kind."

Holt roared out, calling Miggs a fighting name. "You want the man who mistook that damned girl for a young squaw Indian," he said defiantly, "you come and get him. He didn't know that blamed girl was white. She was dressed like a squaw."

"What's that got to do with it, Holt? Red or white, she was still a girl. The feller who hit her, then dumped her because he thought he'd hit her too hard, isn't fit to live, whether she's Indian or white, and I want him."

"You do, do you? Well, damn your Indian-lovin' hide, you just try and get him, Miggs. I'll blow you in two on sight and roast your damned gizzard over my cookin' fire."

Frank came up at this point and shoved groggy Clark Forrester roughly forward. "Go on," McCoy said to the cowboy. "And next time when you're figuring to sneak up and bushwhack somebody, don't try it on grown men or you just might lose your curly top knot."

Forrester saw Miggs and glared, but his face was pale. Obviously Clark Forrester had a headache; the point of his jaw was badly swelling and turning purple.

Miggs jerked his head peremptorily. Forrester started off through the trees. Miggs called out again.

"Forrester's coming, Holt! Turn Brian loose!"

There was no acknowledgement of this. For a moment Jack and Frank thought Holt had decided not to free Brian. In fact, McCoy was just opening up with some blistering invective when Fred Brian came up none too steadily toward them through the trees. His hat was gone, his hip holster was empty, and his shirt was torn, exposing a bloody upper arm and left shoulder.

They took him back where Morton and Murphy waited. Frank and Red went after their horses while Red and Jack Miggs sat down with Brian.

"It was a foolish thing to try, I reckon," mumbled Hyatt Tolman's range boss. "But after I saw Beverly . . . After we walked out in the moonlight last night, I couldn't rest for thinking about the man who did that to her."

Miggs picked up a pine needle, popped it into his mouth, and quietly masticated. After a while he said, quietly and softly: "To tell you the truth, Fred, I had something about like that in the back of my mind, too. Only you beat me to it." He spat out the pine needle. "Tell me, how'd you happen to get captured?"

"The old man's son was standing guard in the trees. They'd been expecting trouble. It was dark, Jackson. I didn't even see him until he'd thrown down on me."

"And how'd you get loose?"

"They tied my hands. I had all night to worry that rope until it stretched. The hell of it was, every man

128

jack of 'em sleeps with his guns. Otherwise, if I could've gotten my hands on a weapon, I'd have killed Bert when he trailed me."

Miggs turned to look squarely into Brian's eyes. "Why Bert?" he gently asked, already knowing the answer to his own question.

"Because Bert was the one who got Bev. That's why!"

CHAPTER
FOURTEEN

On the way back to Miggs's meadow by a careful and circuitous route, Fred Brian told them that Denver Holt had ordered the roundup they'd witnessed the night before, after his son had captured Brian. He also told them that Holt had given that order after Fred had explained to the men of Holt's camp why he was stalking them.

"Up to that time," Brian went on, "Bert hadn't told his paw about trying to steal Beverly. But after I explained to him that that was what had brought me over there, old Denver sat across the campfire, glaring at his son. They had words, I'm sure of that, but not while I was around. I think the old man took Bert off away from the others to give him hell."

"That makes me dislike Denver Holt a little less," spoke up Frank McCoy. "At least he wasn't favorable to what his boy had tried to do to Beverly."

Brian shook his head at this, his expression grim and unrelenting. "You're wrong, Frank. The old man didn't care about Beverly or what Bert tried to do. He said so while we were all at the fire. What angered him was the probability that you and Jack . . . all of us . . . would come a-gunning. He said it was bad enough to get run off the Laramie Plains for some killing Bert was involved in, but it was worse causing trouble up in here, because they couldn't go on driving their herd from one place to another indefinitely."

"But they're going to pull out," said Red Morton. "Otherwise, why did they make their gather?"

Fred shrugged. "No one said. All I know is that Denver ordered the cattle rounded up."

Miggs, watching Brian's tanned, handsome face, said: "You don't think they're pulling out, do you, Fred?"

Brian shook his head. "Denver Holt said we were a bunch of scum . . . that they had nothing to worry about from us. No, I've got no idea what he ordered that gather for, Jackson, but I don't think they're leaving the Ute Peak country."

For a while the five of them rode along. Frank McCoy stuffed his little pipe, lit it, and thoughtfully puffed before saying: "Fred, a man's got to be some kind of a fool to attempt what you tried to do."

McCoy puffed on, watching Brian's expression closely. When Brian's answer to this came back, Frank heeded it, kept on puffing, and got an almost serene look on his face.

"I reckon I was a fool, Frank. I won't deny that. But I had a good reason."

They got back to the meadow, cared for their horses, and broke up — part of them heading for the cow camp, Miggs and McCoy walking tiredly along toward the cabin. It was early evening, balmy, fragrant, and velvet-shadowed.

"You heard what he said about why he tried that!" exclaimed McCoy to Miggs. "Now I'd say a man who'd be that blamed stupid's just got to sure-fire admire the girl he did that for."

Miggs said nothing, neither did he look around. He walked almost to the cabin door before halting. "A hell of a lot of good he'd be to her dead, Frank, and that's what he almost was."

McCoy removed his pipe, knocked it empty, carefully pocketed it before he said scoffingly: "Pshaw, now you're talking like a man who doesn't want anything to happen to Brian. Last night out here you didn't talk that way at all."

Miggs darkly scowled. Most other men would have felt the yeasty disapproval of that black look, but not Frank McCoy.

In the same careless way Frank said: "It's all right, Jack. Hell's bells, I'm on your side. I want what's best for her, too. But I think maybe your being a brand-new father and all . . . sort of . . . you might be just a wee bit overprotective."

Behind them the cabin door opened, Beverly stepped out, saw those two shadows, and went quietly over to look first into McCoy's face, then into Jackson Miggs's face.

"Where did all of you disappear to?" she asked of Miggs. "When I got up this morning to start breakfast, there wasn't a soul anywhere around."

Miggs's brows smoothed out. He made a crooked little smile and said: "Well, how about supper . . . have you got that ready?"

Beverly's white teeth flashed in the dusk. "I can have it ready in a jiffy." She started to turn, stopped, looked over at McCoy, and said: "Uncle Frank, where did you go?"

Frank told her. He felt Miggs's disapproving stare on him, but, as Frank had once said, Beverly Shafter was now a big girl. In Frank McCoy's philosophy of life you looked the bitter as squarely in the face as you also looked at the pleasant. He didn't believe in glossing over harshness, for life was seldom easy, and those who hesitated in a crisis or who shrank from meeting violence with violence, usually went down into the ground before they'd had much chance to cast a shadow among the living.

When he finished, Beverly's liquid eyes were large and shades darker than usual. "Was he hurt?" she asked, speaking of Fred Brian. "Uncle Frank . . . was he hurt?"

"Roughed up a mite is all, and, if you ask me, I'll tell you he had that coming to him, riding off all alone like that, and for such a silly reason."

Beverly stiffened her full length.

Miggs saw the flare of abrupt anger in her eyes and it surprised him. He had never before seen her temper and in fact would have scoffed if anyone had told him anyone as sweet and pretty and tiny as she was could possess a temper.

"A silly reason! Uncle Frank, what Fred did actually was . . ."

"Yes, what was it, Bev?"

"It was *noble*, that's what it was. And you have no right to say he had that coming, whatever it was those men did to him."

"Your arm and head must be a lot better tonight," drawled McCoy, letting this wrathful blast break over him without heeding it. "And say, isn't that the dress we bought just before we left Laramie? I thought you said you only figured to wear it on very special . . ."

"He might be hurt internally for all you know. For all you care." Bev paused. She was breathing hard. Her flashing gaze swung to include Jackson Miggs. Just for a moment it looked as though she might apportion Miggs some of her anger, too, but in the end she did not, she simply whirled away from those two men and went running southward down toward the cow camp.

For a while Miggs and McCoy stood there gazing out where the little cooking fire of Tolman's riders danced and writhed against the purple night.

"You did that on purpose," Miggs said to McCoy, without looking at Frank. "You deliberately made her mad."

"Yup," agreed McCoy cheerily. "Jack, I could talk to you about how the wind's blowin' between Bev and Fred Brian until I was plumb black in the face, and you'd doubt me all the way."

Miggs nodded slowly, gravely. "I understand," he murmured, shook himself out of his reverie, and went over, pushed back the cabin door, and, looking back, said: "Frank, you're the most devious, calculating old reprobate I've ever known. The only thing that's in your favor is that you don't use your slyness to hurt folks."

The pair of them went on inside. McCoy glumly surveyed the cold stove, the hanging pots, and growled: "Well, I sure don't benefit myself sometimes at all. Now I reckon she won't be back for a couple of hours, and here we stand with our bellies flap empty."

Miggs closed the front door, went over to the stove, and began working up their nighttime meal. He had nothing to say until he'd set the table, spooned elk stew into two tin plates, poured the coffee, and motioned McCoy forward to eat.

Then he said: "Frank, why did Holt gather those cussed Durhams of his if, as Fred says, he isn't aiming on leaving the country?"

McCoy ate ravenously, slurped down hot black coffee, and shrugged. "That's Holt's worry, not ours, so eat up, Jack. Eat up."

"It's a riddle. He's not the kind of a cowman to push his critters around a lot unless he's got a plumb good reason."

McCoy raised a saturnine face. "Forget it. I'll give you something better to worry about, if you just plain got to worry. I wouldn't bet a plugged dollar Brian doesn't try riding over there again, only this time with Red and Lex."

Miggs's distant, probing look this time vanished. He brought his eyes down and around in a big sweep, settled them flintily upon McCoy, and grimly shook his head. "No you don't," he growled. "You don't get me all upset again, dog-gone you."

McCoy smacked his lips, raffishly smiled, lifted his tin cup, and emptied it. "Tell me one thing, Jack. Exactly what solid objection have you got to Bev and Fred Brian being interested in one another?"

"Well . . . I don't rightly know, Frank. None really, I reckon, only she's so young."

"He's a good boy and he's got guts. Maybe not a whole lot of sense. Now, neither you nor me'd have tried bracing that whole crew like he did just over a husky little girl."

Miggs looked at Frank. McCoy's expression was sly again; he was deliberately leading Miggs along to a rash statement. Miggs recognized this and said: "That's not true and you know it isn't. If he hadn't gone over there, either you or I would have."

McCoy's sly look faded. He slowly nodded, his gaze still upon Miggs. "All right, then he was noble, like she said he was, and he's got guts. Those are pretty good virtues in my eyes."

"Dog-gone you, Frank," snapped Miggs, then paused, finished his coffee, and leaned forward with both elbows upon the table. "All right. I've got *no* objections. Is that what you want me to say?"

"It is."

"I said it. Now what?"

Frank rummaged for his little pipe. "Nothing, Jack. Nothing at all. Now we just keep our long noses out of it and sort of sit back and see what happens between 'em. You got a match?"

Jack tossed one over, watched Frank light up, lean back, and contentedly puff. "You good and comfortable?" he asked.

"Never been more comfortable, Jack."

"That's good, because since I got the supper, your chore is to clean up the dishes."

Jack got up, went over to dig out his own pipe, stuff it, and go back to the table and also light up. The pair of them sat for a long quiet moment just gazing at one another.

McCoy chuckled deep down, heaved upright, and leaned upon the table, his eyes dancing affectionately. He did not speak a single word, yet something gentle and yet entirely masculine passed back and forth between McCoy and Miggs.

Out in the quiet night a long distance off a cow bawled. This sound came down the stillness without any echo. Another sound, much farther out, also briefly broke the stillness — the sad, mournful tonguing of a wolf as he sat alone howling at the lop-sided old pewter moon that was serenely floating overhead.

Miggs went to his washstand, considered his unshaven, unkempt condition, and prepared to rectify this by taking down the new straight razor McCoy had brought him.

As he worked at this, and as Frank passed back and forth from table to dishpan, Miggs said: "Frank, if Holt had come out and said he'd leave me alone, instead of telling me to keep away from *him*, maybe I'd believe he was leaving the country with his Durhams. But I've been turning that over in my mind and I think he's up to something."

McCoy turned, leaned upon the cooling stove, and spoke around the little pipe tightly clamped between his teeth. "Funny you should mention Holt. I was thinking of him, too . . . him and his boy."

Miggs swung around, one side of his face lathered with white. He put an intent look on Frank. "Now don't you go getting any ideas about riding over and settling up for Bev. One *noble* tomfool around here is enough."

"Why I wasn't thinking that at all, Jack. I was thinking that, if Fred's noble, what's wrong with *both* you and me being noble, also?"

Miggs, with that glistening razor hanging in mid-air, remained entirely still for a long time before he turned back toward the mirror again. "Sometimes," he murmured as he shaved, "you come up with a rare good idea, Frank. Suppose we were to put out the lamp in an hour or such matter . . . after Beverly's returned and gone to bed . . . then just up and did that, just up and slipped out of here."

"Tell you one thing," said McCoy. "Won't any of that rough, tough crew walk up behind us two like they did young Brian."

"They'll be watching, though."

"Sure they will, Jack. It'd be sort of disappointing if they weren't watching."

Miggs went on with his shaving. Nothing more was said for a long time. Not until McCoy had finished cleaning up once Jack himself was through, when

138

somewhere out in the night, up by the pole gate across the horse cañon's mouth, a tinkle of rich, warm laughter came down the soft night air to bring those older men around, slowly listening and exchanging a long look.

"That was Bev," pronounced Frank.

"I'm not deaf," growled Miggs, looking bleak.

"I don't figure she'd ought to be out there alone with Brian like that. It's not . . . well . . . lady-like."

"What d'you know about what's lady-like and what isn't?" McCoy asked, smiling while draping a dish towel between two nails behind the stove. "Besides, how's a feller going to do his courting with old grannies like you and me shooing all the little chicks back under the old hen's wings come sundown?"

Miggs crossed to where his rifle stood beside the door, picked the weapon up, returned to the table with it, and frowningly started cleaning the gun.

McCoy watched this for a while, then also took his rifle to the table and worked over it.

"What would old Jed Shafter say, do you reckon," he asked Miggs, "if he saw his girl tonight?"

Jack looked up, his dead-level smoky eyes perplexed. "Don't know," he eventually said. "I can't picture Jed having a girl like that at all."

"And he," observed McCoy shrewdly, "would probably have the same trouble trying to picture you being father or foster father to a girl like that."

Miggs resumed working on his gun. He seemed to have gone off on some private thought trail of his own now, which suited McCoy just fine, because all he'd meant to do was divert Miggs's attention from those two lovers out in the night.

A horned owl around back somewhere began its nocturnal hooting. This mysterious and lonely sound persisted, at spaced intervals, for perhaps ten minutes. Finally, when it stopped, the hush was deeper than ever.

Miggs finished with his gun. Frank likewise finished but he refilled his shell belt instead of just sitting there, and after a while he said: "Come on, let's go. We don't have to wait for Bev anyway."

CHAPTER
FIFTEEN

The night was composed of several things — the dying, curling light from down at the cow camp, the great, curving overhead sky with its myriad diamond-like small lights, and the good, safe aroma from two cooking fires.

There was something else, too, but neither Jackson Miggs nor Frank McCoy let on to the other that they were aware of this as they passed on silent, moccasined feet around behind the cabin northward toward the dark forest. There were two vague silhouettes up by the horse cañon pole gate, one tall, one quite short and sturdy.

Miggs slowed almost to a halt as he glided on past those two closely standing shadows by the pole gate. Frank gave him a rough nudge, but Miggs did not pick up the gait at all. If anything, he seemed to slow still more.

"Leave 'em be," hissed McCoy. "Besides, if they see us out here with our guns, they'll know . . ."

"They wouldn't see us right now, Frank, if we was to burst down upon them with scalping knives."

Miggs halted finally, watching those two silhouettes. He settled his gun butt into the ground, hooked both massive arms around the weapon, and leaned there, saying nothing, just watching.

"This isn't decent," objected McCoy in a bleak whisper. "You're not supposed to spy on folks like this, Jack. It's downright indecent."

Miggs remained rooted and totally silent.

"Come on, consarn it, we haven't got all night to get over to Holt's camp and back."

Still Miggs did not move.

McCoy finally gave it up, leaned upon his own gun, and also watched.

Fred was clean-shaven and attired in a fresh, clean, blue work shirt. He was hatless in the silver glow of moonlight. He stood less than a foot from Beverly, gazing down at her. He said: "I'd do it over again. Even if you didn't mean as much to me as you do, I'd still do it over again."

She murmured something in reply to this but it was not entirely distinguishable from where Jack and Frank stood in formless tree shadows, looking and listening.

". . . necessary, really, Fred."

"Yes, it was," came back his swift and emphatic reply to this. "He's no good, Beverly, and if it hadn't been you, believe me, it'd have been some other girl. If not up here, then down around one of the settlements. I'm not finished with him, either."

Beverly drew upright. She put a hand upon his arm, saying firmly, loudly enough for Jack and Frank to hear: "Let it go. Please let it go, Fred. I'm all right. It was that bull elk that gashed my arm, not him."

142

"Beverly, if he hadn't thought he'd killed you with that knock over the head, do you know what he'd have done?"

"No, Fred, I don't, and neither do you, because it didn't happen."

"I know, Beverly. I know because I know his kind. And when they had me . . . it was Bert arguing loudest to dump my carcass in a cañon. I owe him something for that, don't I?"

She raised her head to him, shook it gently from side to side, and murmured something neither Miggs nor McCoy could hear. Frank fidgeted in his tracks; he was feeling mean about this eavesdropping, but at the same time what was very clearly going to happen thrilled him to the bottom of his raffish old soul.

And it happened. Bev stood up on her tiptoes, leaned into him, and Fred's dark head cut down swiftly to seek her lips.

Frank turned all limp where he was hugging his rifle, and let out a soft, melancholy sigh.

Jack watched that kiss for a moment, turned, squinted, and said: "Frank, didn't that elk stew agree with you? You're looking almighty peaked around the jowls."

McCoy dragged his limpid gaze around, focused it upon Miggs, and very gradually drew upright. "The trouble with you," he pronounced in a loud hiss, "is that you got no romance in your heart, Jackson Miggs."

"But I'm powerful good at tracking," retorted Miggs, returning his glance to where Beverly Shafter and Fred

Brian stood, parted now, quite silent and seeming abashed.

McCoy snorted, cradled his long rifle, and turned away. "You can stay here if you're of a mind to," he snapped, "but me, I've got a long walk and maybe a little brawling to do yet tonight."

Miggs turned, watched McCoy's irate stride for a moment, slyly smiled, and passed on silently behind Frank up into the forest. It appeared that two could play at that game of being cunning, of baiting others.

A half mile later, before either Miggs or McCoy had really gotten into their stride, something large and dark sprang out of a pine needle bed, gave a startling snort, and went charging northward through the forest.

Frank McCoy, in the lead when this happened, almost dropped his rifle and afterward his voice was a squeak.

Miggs, down on one knee and with his rifle snugged back to fire, did not pull the trigger. He very slowly lowered the weapon, very slowly stood upright again, and, although Frank's wild profanity was making concentration difficult, Miggs hearkened to the crashing sounds of that fleeing animal until the beast was lost entirely to sight.

"Danged bull elk!" exclaimed McCoy, his voice coming back down to normal. "Big as a damned tree he was, Jack. Did you see him? Biggest bull I ever saw."

"Bull elk, hell," grumbled Miggs. "And if you'd had your eyes where they'd ought to have been, you wouldn't have stumbled over the thing, either, Frank."

"What d'you mean it wasn't a bull elk . . . why, I saw those two little bloodshot eyes close enough to poke a finger into 'em. Don't you stand there and tell me . . ."

"Well, I *am* telling you, Frank. That was no bull elk."

"Then what the hell was it? Isn't another critter in the mountains that big. His dad-blasted shoulder come even with my . . ."

"That was a big Durham bull."

McCoy let his protests trail off long enough for him to stare at Miggs, to blink at him.

"He was a big devil and he was a muley bull . . . no horns. He'd be one of Denver Holt's critters, Frank."

"This far east?"

"Yes, this far east, and if some of the men we used to know had seen you practically fall over a regular range bull without even seeing it, they'd just about . . ."

"Anyone can have accidents, Jackson Miggs, dog-gone you."

Miggs twisted at the waist, looked upcountry where that big old bull had disappeared, twisted back, and said: "I think I'm beginning to understand about Holt's roundup, Frank. I think we guessed every reason for it but the right one. I don't think he's heading out of the country, at all, and I don't believe he's going westward looking for new range. If that was so, why would one of his bulls be this far east?"

Frank opened his mouth. Miggs cut in ahead of whatever McCoy had meant to say.

"He's coming *east* with his herd. He figures we've got the best grass over here, and he's right about that, too."

"But, hell, Jack . . . Tolman's white-faces are over here."

"Old Holt will know that. He just won't give a damn. Aside from thinking he's entitled to go anywhere he pleases up in here, *he* doesn't care about his cows being bred to Hereford bulls . . . it's Fred Brian and Hyatt Tolman who *don't* want their white-face crosses bred to those shorthorn bulls."

Miggs cradled his rifle, strode firmly on past Frank, and left McCoy to unravel this new trouble at his leisure. Frank did, but he slipped along behind Miggs as he did so, and he kept his eyes constantly moving, too, as he reassumed his westward progress.

They encountered bedded-down cows, calves, young heifers, and even a sifting of short yearling steers. The numbers of Holt's cattle steadily increased until, finally, a little over a mile and a half onward, Miggs halted altogether.

When McCoy came up, looking around at all those uneasy cattle in the inky night, he said: "You're dead right, Jack. Holt's figuring on taking over the country Tolman's been using up in here for many years."

"Trouble," muttered Jackson Miggs more to himself than to McCoy. "Holt's out for trouble. He's not going to ride roughshod over Brian or anyone else up in my country. I don't give a copper-colored damn how tough and rough he thinks he is." Miggs reversed his course and brushed angrily past McCoy.

146

Frank called softly: "What you figure to do?"

"Get Fred, Red, Lex, you, and me on horseback, and at the first sign of daylight push these dog-goned Durhams back west. Come along."

Once more McCoy fell in behind the thoroughly aroused burly man hiking back the way they had come, and had almost to trot to keep up.

By the time they got back to Miggs's meadow neither one of those two silhouettes was still there by the pole gate. But then Frank hadn't expected them to be there because it was now past midnight.

Even the campfire from Brian's cow camp had died to nothing more illuminating than a bed of rusty-red coals.

Miggs hesitated in front of his cabin, looking over that way.

Frank, reading his thoughts, said: "She's abed. Don't worry about her."

They went on down to the cow camp, their movements silent, their silhouettes shadowy and unreal-looking. There, Miggs went from blanket roll to blanket roll until he'd located Brian. He dropped to one knee with his rifle standing straight up beside him and ungently shook Tolman's range boss awake.

Brian sat up, blinked at the grim visage of those two older men hovering over him, ran a hand across his eyes, and straightened his upper body.

In short sentences Miggs told what he and Frank had encountered less than a mile from this very meadow. He also said that he was positive those Durhams were not out there by accident. "My *guess* is that he meant to drive his cattle over here with your critters right from the start, Fred. He's undoubtedly scouted my cabin, the countryside hereabouts, and the amount of feed your critters are grazing on this land. He deliberately bunched his critters yesterday, and, even before the fight, he meant to drive them over here."

Brian ran bent fingers through his hair. "See any bulls among his cattle?" he asked.

McCoy made a loud snort. "See 'em!" he exclaimed. "We stumbled right over one, Fred. Danged critter was a muley, and, so help me, he was bigger'n a saddle horse and three times as heavy. And, boy, he wasn't no more than a long half mile from right here where I'm standing this minute."

Fred heard McCoy out, stopped scratching his head, and looked at Jackson Miggs. "What do you figure we'll have to do?" he asked, and until Fred had said that Miggs had entirely forgotten the trust Hyatt Tolman had put upon him, as well as his own spur-of-the-moment agreement to help Brian with Tolman's cattle.

"Run 'em out of the country," interjected Frank McCoy. "Isn't that what you said out there, Jack?"

Miggs felt trapped; he also felt thoroughly angry. He got up from beside Brian's bedroll and nodded. "That's what we're going to do, too," he rumbled. "Fred, come sunup, saddle a couple of extra horses for Frank and me. The five of us will drift Holt's cattle back westerly where they came from, and this time, if he gets his back up, so help me, he's going to think a whole war party of Utes is breathing down his cussed neck!"

148

Brian nodded, looking enormously relieved. He eased back down in his blankets, watched Miggs's craggy old tough face for a moment, then, in an altogether different tone, he said: "Jackson . . . and you, too, Frank . . . sometime tomorrow I'd like to talk to you fellers off by ourselves if we can. It's got nothing to do with Holt or his Durhams, either."

Miggs dropped his eyes, looking suddenly startled and uneasy. Without acknowledging that he'd heard Brian, he turned toward the cabin, saying roughly — "Come along, Frank." — and strode swiftly away.

Brian scowled faintly as he watched those two older men go along, then he shrugged and lay back, gazing solemnly up at the great vault of heaven.

CHAPTER
SIXTEEN

They left Miggs's meadow before sunup again, each man being particularly careful not to make any unnecessary noise. They brought it off, too, although McCoy hadn't been sure they could, because, after slipping away the morning before, he thought it likely Beverly would be more alert the second time.

But evidently she was deep in dreams. They got completely across the meadow and into the trees without her stepping out of the cabin or even appearing in the doorway.

"So far so good," Frank told Red Morton.

The cowboy nodded without much interest. He didn't know what Frank meant and had other things on his mind, anyway.

They went carefully, with Miggs leading and Fred Brian behind him. Where Miggs and McCoy had encountered the muley bull, they halted long enough for Jackson to make a forward reconnaissance afoot. He came back to say: "The herd's another half mile on ahead. That bull must've struck out on his own last night."

"Yeah," assented Brian dourly. "Probably scented my critters and was heading for them when dark caught up with him."

From behind Brian, McCoy spoke up: "Jack, Holt'll have scouts out sure as the devil."

This warning, while undoubtedly accurate enough, was not something Miggs had been unaware of for some time now. He nodded back at Frank, swung up, and reined southward, leading his companions away from the main part of Holt's Durham herd.

After paralleling the rousing cattle for some twenty minutes, Miggs halted again. This time he drew forth his rifle as he dismounted, jerked his head for the others to do likewise, and motioned for silence.

Red Morton pushed up to whisper: "Jack, this time let Lex mind the stock."

Miggs shrugged, beckoned them all up to him, planted his rifle butt down, and said: "Murphy, you stay with the horses. Whatever happens, don't let 'em set us afoot. If you've got to clear out, ride one horse, and run the others on ahead of you. When it's safe, return to this same spot. Here's where we'll rendezvous. Understand?"

Lex Murphy nodded.

Miggs considered the others a moment before speaking again. "We're in front of Holt's herd," he ultimately said. "If there's much gunfire, they'll likely stampede. Boys, watch out for that. If it happens, shinny up a danged tree and never mind the splinters. There's a lot of Durhams around us in here . . . if you get caught afoot underneath 'em in a stampede, the rest of us'll need spoons to pick up what they leave of you."

"If Holt guesses what we're doing up in here," put in Frank McCoy, "he'll stampede the critters and don't you ever think otherwise."

That point covered, Miggs now gestured right and left with his rifle barrel. "We go walking along northward now, but always keep the feller next to you in your sight. Don't get lost or split up. In a fight among trees you got to know where your friends are, otherwise the wrong fellers can get shot."

Brian gradually scowled. "I thought last night you said we were going to push these cattle back westerly. Now you're talking about a war with Holt's crew."

"It's the same thing," explained Miggs. "When we start walking westward, we'll push the cattle along ahead of us. But unless I've got Denver Holt figured entirely wrong, it's not going to take him long to figure out what's happening. Then the fighting'll start."

"But couldn't we push the cattle along a heap better on horseback, Jackson?"

Miggs's reply, like its accompanying stare, was saturnine. "Yeah, we could," he grunted. "And a man sitting six feet up in the air above a horse makes the pleasantest target you could ask for, too."

Brian said no more. In fact, none of them said any more.

Miggs looked around. When Frank McCoy faintly nodded at him indicating they were ready to proceed, Miggs made another gesture left and right.

"Let's go," he said. "Remember . . . keep one another in sight."

They fanned out as Lex Murphy led their horses back toward a particularly dense tree and brush thicket to the south. They hadn't forged a hundred feet ahead before Frank, to the north, encountered a few cattle stirring up out of their beds. It was still gloomy in this part of the forest. For that matter, although there was gray and watery light out in the open places, the sun itself had not yet arisen.

Frank signaled to the others and walked on toward Holt's Durhams. When the animals saw a man appear suddenly and noiselessly among them, on foot, they sprang up with frantic grunts and broke away westward.

Red Morton and Fred Brian came upon other bedded critters. So did Miggs farther south. As the four of them pushed ahead in their long skirmish line, Durham cattle sprang up and fled back westerly, first in isolated little advance pockets, then, after a while, in large numbers.

It was obvious to all of them that except for the fight yesterday afternoon, which had delayed Holt for several hours, his herd would have been as far east as Miggs's meadow by this time. As it was, Holt and his men had evidently stopped the drive when it became too dark in the forest after sundown, left the critters to bed down wherever blackness overtook them, and had themselves left to camp far back, probably, Miggs thought, in open country where they could keep sharp watch roundabout.

By the time Miggs's line had advanced a quarter mile dust was beginning to thicken again in the air from all those retreating Durham cattle. There was considerable

153

disturbed lowing but no frightened, alarm-sounding bawling as yet.

Miggs paused once to put his gaze northward for as long as it took to see and identify Fred, Red, and Frank. It was important the four of them did not get split up.

Satisfied then, he started onward once more, had progressed perhaps a hundred yards, when he was brought up short by the questioning nicker of a horse not far ahead, and a little south of him. Others evidently had also heard that horse, for at once four men passed from sight around behind nearby big pine trees.

Miggs waited for the horse to repeat his call but he never did. However, a man's garrulous voice was lifted now, sounding annoyed and drowsy.

Miggs thought he knew what was happening; the numbers of those retreating cattle had possibly awakened one of Holt's men out ahead in the meadow. Whoever that man was, he could by this time see hundreds of Durhams walking westward back out of the easterly forest, and perhaps he was as yet too sleepy to realize something had to have started those cattle withdrawing to the west. Possibly, because the animals were neither frightened nor in any big hurry, he conceivably thought it was just one of those spontaneous things cattle often times do.

In any event, that cowboy roused himself to full wakefulness, blasted out a big curse, and called upon Holt's other men to rise up, to get their horses, and turn the herd back. This man also called indignantly for someone Miggs thought was the night guard. The reason Miggs thought this was because that irate rider heaped imprecations upon someone on ahead as though that man should have seen what was happening first.

Fred Brian stepped forth from behind a tree, caught Miggs's attention, and made a rushing motion, evidently to convey the meaning that he thought they should all rush out upon Holt's camp before it was fully awake.

Miggs agreed with this, but made a motion back to Brian indicating that Fred should wait. Miggs then left his own tree, soundlessly slipping forward toward the forest's edge to study the onward land.

He saw at once, though, that it was too late to rush Holt's camp. In the midst of all those withdrawing cattle out upon yonder meadow, made vague by dust and disturbance, men were frantically rigging out saddle horses, calling back and forth, and cursing at the Durhams streaming past.

There was still the element, if not entirely of surprise, then at least of diversion, though, for Holt and his men as yet were too fully occupied to pay attention to the possibility that this withdrawal of the cattle from the easterly forest was not spontaneous. But even as Miggs considered his next course of action, a dense throng of Durhams piled up around Holt's frantic men out there, and someone — Miggs knew immediately who — blasted off a thunderous gunshot that panicked the closely packed Durhams.

Where that rifle bullet struck at the heels of the most easterly cattle, it flung sharp particles of gravelly soil against tender legs and flanks. This stinging, as well as that whip-sawing fierce explosion, did what Frank McCoy had obviously meant for it to do. Cattle sprang ahead, struck other cattle, horns clicked, and bulging dark eyes swung aimlessly in wild panic. In a moment the rush was on. It transmitted itself to the other animals. Some were able to swing wide around that small pocket of yelling men in the dark, heaving sea of tawny brown hides. Others, running blind as stampeding cattle invariably do, swept in and over Holt's camp, upsetting cooking pots, snagging bedroll blankets on wickedly tipped horns, and forcing Holt's men to dive every which way for safety's sake.

Miggs had not thought of stampeding the cattle, but now that it was done he kneeled, took careful aim, and fired a thunderous shot of his own. Again, a bullet sent stinging gravel against those straining, rearmost animals.

Other guns opened up from the forest fringe, kicking dirt and stones to whizzing life behind the running cattle. Miggs reloaded and hung there on one knee waiting to get in another shot. He was not able to do this, though, because of the dust and wild confusion upon the meadow.

Frank appeared beside him. He dropped down, put his lips up to Miggs's ear, and called loudly over the yelling and bawling and earth-shaking thunder of all those stampeding hoofs.

"Run in behind the cattle!" Frank said a little breathlessly. "If we stay close enough, they can't see us, let alone get a shot at us. We can finish the lot of 'em."

Miggs shook his head. That tumult out there was too loud to be shouted over now, so he simply raised one arm and pointed, showing McCoy that, trampled, taken by surprise and reeling from their punishment or not, Denver Holt's men were not losing their heads. They were doing precisely the only thing that could have saved them under those circumstances. They were running *with* the cattle, not against them. In this way they were beyond a doubt saving their lives, but, as far as Frank's scheme was concerned, they were also, perhaps unknowingly, getting out of the meadow while dozens of orry-eyed cattle were between them and their attackers, making it impossible for anyone to down them with gunfire.

Frank watched as did the others. Red and Fred Brian drifted down to join Frank and Jack Miggs. None of them had anything to say for as long as that panoply of wild confusion existed out across the meadow. Two of Holt's men had managed to hang onto their terrified horses. Those two got dragged along, belly down, for five or six hundred feet, then one of the men let go. The second cowboy managed to hook both heels against an upthrust boulder, set himself, and stop his horse although the abrupt force of his stopping the animal tumbled the rider end over end. That rider managed to get astride.

The watchers caught glimpses of him now and then when he passed from one dust cloud to another, wisely allowing the fleeing cattle to carry him and his horse along.

"Big gamble," said Red Morton from lips that scarcely moved. "If them cattle knock that horse down, he's a goner. They'll cut him to ribbons under all them hoofs."

No one commented. Every one of them knew exactly how true Morton's observation was. Once, when that man passed out into view, Frank McCoy and Jackson Miggs exchanged a look; either one of them could have downed that man with their rifles. The range was much too great for carbines, but not for those long-barreled mountaineer rifles they carried.

"Frank?" called Miggs, and kept his grave gaze upon McCoy.

Frank looked far out, puckered his brow, narrowed his eyes, and pulled his mouth down at its outer corners. "You!" he called back. "I'm not up to it."

Miggs smiled.

Frank, seeing that look, also smiled. He also ruefully wagged his head back and forth. "Don't quite have the stomach for it," he said. "You, Jack?"

Miggs shook his head, swung back, and watched that cowboy riding for his life amid all those heaving, shaggy brown bodies and clashing, wicked horns. He had no idea which of Holt's men it was, out there, and right then he didn't care. Anyone who thought that fast, that clearly, to stay alive, deserved at least to survive the stampede.

Whatever that man got himself involved in afterward would be another affair entirely. But here and now, in

Jackson Miggs's view as well as in Frank McCoy's thoughts, that man was entitled to victory, if he could achieve it, without being interfered with from behind when he could not possibly protect himself from any more peril than he was right then in the midst of.

Miggs, feeling eyes upon him, looked up and around. Both Morton and Fred Brian were looking at him and at his rifle, their expressions obvious. Miggs shrugged and looked away from them, returning his attention to where the fleeing man had finally made it safely in among the westerly growth of shielding trees.

CHAPTER
SEVENTEEN

Holt's cattle had fled on into the forest without any slackening of their stride. In among them somewhere were Holt's battered men, all but one of them afoot, and probably, as Frank observed to Jackson Miggs, if not injured, then at least badly knocked around.

"So let's keep the advantage," Frank said as Miggs stood up.

Miggs checked his rifle, then gazed over at Red Morton. "Go get Lex and fetch back the horses," he said calmly. When Red darted away, Miggs swung toward McCoy. "Calm down. We're going after them. Just simmer down, Frank."

Murphy came back with Red mounted beside him. They handed down the reins to Brian, McCoy, and Miggs, and afterward trailed along behind Miggs who led the lot of them on around the churned-up meadow where dust still hung in the morning air.

Beyond the meadow, to the west, they encountered some run-out, panting cattle. These beasts stared stupidly as the riders went past, making no move to run; they were exhausted and some of them were hurt where they'd struck head-on into trees or had been knocked down and trampled by the other critters.

160

Miggs swung his head, saying: "Guns out and ready."

That was all he had to say. They were now in the vicinity where they could expect to encounter Denver Holt and his men. In fact, they were past two of Holt's cowboys without even knowing it. And they didn't know it until a man let off a cry of alarm behind them and to the north, and fired at them.

Frank McCoy, farthest back, left his saddle in a soaring leap, hit down hard, and rolled like a ball to get behind a tree. The others also swung down on the fly. Miggs, anxiously looking back to see whether Frank had voluntarily left the saddle or had been shot out of it, saw Frank press in close to the tree, put aside his rifle, remove his floppy old hat, and solemnly poke a finger through a little round hole in the crown that had not been there before. Then Frank swore with feeling.

Miggs motioned for Red and Frank to circle around across from him. He slipped up where Fred Brian was stiffly standing, said — "Cover me from here." — and slipped away again, bound northward in the direction from which that single shot had come.

The smell of cattle, of dust, of strife and turmoil, was rank among the trees. Sounds of cattle floated back downcountry from where the Durhams were running themselves out through the westerly forest. Once, a man's bull-bass roar sounded waveringly far ahead. Miggs recognized that voice and was gratified that Denver Holt was not still back here where at least two of his men were making a stand on foot.

Frank McCoy's rifle roared.

Miggs stepped behind a tree, looked back, saw the puff of dirty smoke from McCoy's black-powder ammunition, swung, and sought for the target Frank had fired at. He did not find it, but he knew Frank well enough to know McCoy would not fire unless he had an enemy in his sights, so, until this was clarified, he remained motionless and hidden.

From off to the east a carbine roared. Miggs placed that gun immediately. When another carbine shot exploded from this same gun, Miggs knew exactly where Red Morton was hiding, but he still could see nothing ahead.

He shunted from his tree to a more forward and distant pine, then sighted what the others had seen. Two men were down flat behind an ancient old deadfall pine. One would raise up, fire, drop down, and his companion would then repeat this maneuver. The second time those cowboys did that Jack recognized them both; one was the curly-headed big man who had been tartly amused at being caught, flat-footed, that time when Miggs and McCoy had captured them on horseback. The other cowboy was Clark Forrester, Holt's youngest and most hot-headed rider. Both were hatless and Forrester's shirt was torn, evidently the result of his bad moments in the midst of the stampede. Both men were firing with six-guns. Neither, it seemed, had Winchesters with them. If the fight was not entirely uneven before, in Miggs's view, it certainly was now. Either he or Frank McCoy could stand up in full view of both those embattled cowboys

162

with their long-barreled rifles, and pick Forrester and his companion off from beyond handgun range.

"Hold it!" Miggs called forward. "You two over there . . . behind that deadfall . . . quit shooting!"

Instead of compliance Miggs harvested a savage flurry of bullets that struck all around the tree that served as his shield. He waited out this storm, then called out again, only this time addressing his companions.

"Frank, hold up a minute! You, too, Red and Fred. All of you, hold up a minute. Give 'em a chance to quit."

"Quit hell!" roared back the knife-edged, furious voice of young Clark Forrester. "Come and get us, you bunch of bushwhackers!"

Miggs kneeled, eased around the tree, raised his rifle, and snugged it back. He took a hand rest and waited. For a while there was not a sound anywhere around. Even that uproar to the west, where the stampede was diminishing, was too far off now to be heard as more than a very faint echo.

Miggs kept his vigil. Time ran on. The sun popped up around a shoulder of aloof Ute Peak in the northward background, and a flashing ray of light shone off blue steel over the trunk of that deadfall. Miggs fired.

A man's involuntary howl shattered the stillness. A blue steel, Colt six-gun whipped straight upward and backward where dust, slivers, and rotting tree trunk exploded under the violent impact.

Frank McCoy's unmistakable keening cry of exultation rang out. "You did it, Jack!" he cried. "You put one of 'em out of commission."

Frank would have exulted even more, but a waspish six-gun shot whipped around the deadfall's eastern-most end, driving Frank back to cover with a yelp. On westward from Frank two youthful voices broke out into derisive profanity as McCoy shrilly denounced the man who had narrowly missed him.

Even Miggs grinned at Frank's indignation. He lowered his rifle, carefully reloaded it, placed it across his left arm, and called out again.

"You boys are pinned down! You can't win and you dassn't run, so why not just quit? That way, at least, you'll end up alive!"

No reply came back to this plea.

Miggs deduced from this, since always before it had been Forrester who had shouted back, that the man he'd incapacitated was indeed Denver Holt's youngest rider.

"All right, boys!" he called. "If they can't see where this'll lead 'em, I reckon we'll have to show them!"

At once two weapons opened up from around eastward where McCoy and Red Morton were. Fred Brian, who had been quite silent throughout all this, now slipped down where Miggs was, got under cover, and said: "That was Forrester you knocked out, Jackson. That other one . . . the big, dark feller . . . is called Curly. Curly Hogston. He was the one who balked hardest about dumping me in a cañon. Let me talk to him. This way, he's going to get killed."

Miggs nodded, bawled over for Frank McCoy and Red Morton to hold their fire. When it was still again, he nodded over at Brian.

"Go ahead. But we've got to end this thing one way or another pretty fast. Holt will have heard the gunfire by now. He'll likely be coming back."

Brian leaned his Winchester aside, cupped both hands to his mouth, and called out.

"Hey, Hogston! This is Fred Brian. I owe you a favor for standing up to the others yesterday. I'm repaying it now. Put down your gun and come out from behind the tree. You're a goner if you don't."

No reply came back even after the last echo had faded out.

Fred stood there, looking hopeful right up to the last. He eventually turned to gaze out of troubled eyes at Miggs.

"I'll try again," he said.

Miggs shrugged, his face stony. "Go ahead, but I don't think Hogston's going to give up. Once more . . . then we'll smoke them out."

Brian cupped his hands again. "Hogston, listen to me! There are two men east of you. They're going on around where they can flank you from behind. There are two men here with rifles, not carbines. Either one of 'em can pick you off farther than your six-gun'll reach. Don't be a fool . . . throw out your gun and call it quits."

This time the trapped cowboy called back an answer. "Brian? Forrester's comin' out. He's hurt. He can't fight any more, so he's comin' out. Hold your fire. All right?"

"All right!" sang out Jackson Miggs, shifting both his stance and his grip on his rifle. "Hey, Morton . . . you and Frank hold off."

A man rose up from behind the deadfall pine. He was holding his right hand and wrist, which were wrapped in a bandanna, with his left hand. Even from pistol-range distance Miggs and Fred could see the anguish in that man's dirty, sweaty face. It was young Forrester. He shuffled on around the deadfall and started unsteadily across the intervening distance.

Miggs kept him covered until he was satisfied Forrester had no weapons. He said to Brian: "Get him, Fred. Check him for a hide-out gun."

Brian met Forrester in among the trees, halted him to search for weapons, and afterward, having found no gun, herded Forrester back where Miggs was. Those two exchanged a long flinty stare.

Miggs put aside his rifle. "How bad's your arm?" he asked.

Forrester snarled: "I'll live, squawman."

Miggs's iron jaw snapped closed. He reached out, caught Forrester by the shirt, lifted him one-handed, and brought Forrester's face up to within three inches of his own face.

"*Mister Miggs*, sonny. Let's hear you say that . . . *Mister Miggs*."

Forrester, astonished at the power of Jackson's mighty right arm, said in a faint whisper: "*Mister Miggs*."

166

Brian took over when Miggs flung the cowboy from him. "What'll it take to get Hogston out from behind that danged log?" he asked.

Forrester dragged his gaze away from Jackson Miggs with an effort. He looked out beyond where Fred Brian stood, to that old deadfall, lifted his shoulders, and let them fall.

"I don't know. You can't scare him out . . . not Curly Hogston. He don't scare worth a damn."

Miggs took up his rifle. "We've wasted enough time," he told Brian. "Take that little nit back where the horses are. Tie him with a lariat and let Murphy patch him up. Go on."

After Forrester and Fred were gone, Miggs drew a careful bead upon the old deadfall about where he thought Hogston would be hiding, and fired. A large hunk of rotted wood burst into powder fine dust, cascading down the deadfall's far side. At once a carbine and another rifle also punished that old tree. Pieces of punk wood flew in several directions and dun-brown dust hung in the air above the deadfall.

For a long time Hogston made no attempt to fire back. When he did fire, though, it was easterly, the way Miggs was sure Red Morton and perhaps Frank McCoy would be moving around him. This surmise was proved correct almost before Hogston's gunfire echo had diminished. First a carbine, then a rifle, exploded off in the direction Hogston had fired. Miggs did not see either of those slugs strike the deadfall, so he assumed that Frank and Red had succeeded in flanking Hogston.

There could now be no hope at all for Denver Holt's curly-headed cowboy. Even if he could hold Red Morton off, he could not hope to do the same with McCoy's long-barreled rifle.

"Hogston!" he shouted. "You've got about half a minute now to make up your mind to die right there or quit! How about it . . . you coming out or not?"

"Why don't you come and get me?" challenged Holt's cowboy.

Miggs's eyes narrowed in thought. There was no way he could frontally approach that deadfall pine without Hogston seeing him, but, if he could do as Frank and Red had done — get around the old log — he could slip through the trees and catch Hogston from the rear. This would take more time than he thought they had, but on the other hand he had no stomach for murdering a brave man, which Hogston obviously was, and which also was bound to happen if he persisted in fighting the odds lined up against him. Miggs sighed, ruefully shook his head, stood up, and started in an eastern direction around through the forest.

He made it to the upper end of Hogston's deadfall, glimpsed something ragged and lumpy crouched midway down the old log's shielding length, caught the flash of sunlight off gun metal, and continued silently along until he was almost directly behind the crouched, straining cowboy. Hogston was swinging his head, trying to watch for another glimpse of men eastward, and also southward where Miggs had been. His face was scratched, his clothing torn, and hair hung sweatily down across his forehead. He was beaten every way but in spirit.

Miggs's moccasined feet made absolutely no sound as he glided up to within fifty feet of the besieged range rider. He stood poised behind a stalwart tree, raised his rifle, took a long sighting, held his breath, and fired. Hogston's right hand with its fisted six-gun was upon the deadfall, stretched out from the rest of him. Miggs's bullet struck the six-gun where the ejector slide and cylinder joined. The gun was violently wrenched from Hogston's fingers.

Miggs leaned his rifle upon the tree and watched Hogston recoil from that numbing blow, watched him flop over upon his back, staring with big eyes straight at Jackson Miggs.

Without a sound, Hogston then sprang up. He was a big man, easily twenty-five years younger than Jackson Miggs, and he was killing mad now. He let out a roar and lunged forward.

Miggs, fearful Morton or Frank McCoy might fire now, stayed back until the very last moment, then stepped straight out into the path of that oncoming big man, braced himself, and ducked under a savage blow Hogston aimed at him. At the same time he cried out: "Hold it, Frank! Don't shoot!"

Hogston whipped past, came around, and launched himself a second time at Jackson Miggs. As before, the older, much heavier, and broader man braced forward, refusing to take a single backward step.

This time they met in a collision that sent reverberations as far away as McCoy and Morton, who were hastening up, but not recklessly, not without utilizing all the cover available because they also knew Denver Holt was probably hurrying back to participate in this battle.

Hogston lashed at Miggs with the full force of his lunging drive. He missed, though, and fell into Miggs. This was Curly Hogston's biggest mistake yet. He realized it the second both those immense arms closed around his upper body, locked behind Hogston's back in a bear-like hug, and slowly, inexorably began to tighten.

Hogston had never heard the legend of Jackson Miggs out-bear-hugging the bear. In fact he'd never heard of Jackson Miggs at all, but now he surmised he was up against no ordinary man. He rained futile blows down upon Miggs's head; he whipped and sawed and threw himself first one way, and then another. None of it helped. Miggs's constricting arms were slowly squeezing the life out of him. Hogston's eyes aimlessly rolled, his mouth flew open, his face became purple, and his flailing fists heaved about and finally fell away altogether.

Miggs, standing wide-legged and braced, suddenly released his hold.

Hogston fell, limp and broken, his eyelids twitching, his nostrils distended.

Red and Frank came up, halted, and gazed downward. McCoy seemed the least appalled of the two.

Morton looked up and down again. "Be damned," he whispered. "He done bear-hugged this one senseless. Or is he plumb dead?"

"Not dead," pronounced McCoy, watching Jackson Miggs go back after his rifle. "But all the same, Red, you'd best use his belt, and your belt, too, and tie his arms behind him."

Red dropped down and Frank bent low to supervise, which was all that kept one or the other of them from being killed, for out of the westerly forest a Winchester roared and a moment later a second Winchester exploded.

Miggs, back with his rifle, dropped as though he'd been shot, whipped up his gun, and fired at movement in the gloomy distance. Up ahead, someone yelped.

Down beside Hogston, Frank McCoy squeaked at Morton. "Go on, boy, tie him up, dammit. Never mind the Holts, Jack and I'll fix their red wagon for 'em. Tie him up, and then slap him back to his senses and take him on back where Brian went with that other one. Go on, boy, do like I say . . . move!"

CHAPTER
EIGHTEEN

After Jackson Miggs's snap shot up into the gloomy forest shadows where those two carbines had opened up on McCoy and Morton when they were bending over Curly Hogston, there was a long lull.

During it Frank called over quietly to Miggs, saying: "The Holts, Jack. By my calculations there should be three men up in there."

"I think only two now," Miggs answered back. "I winged someone . . . I heard him squeal." Miggs was well hidden. He turned now carefully, considering the westerly forest. "Frank, stay down where you are. I'll slip on toward 'em. You give me cover fire."

McCoy bobbed his head up and down, pressed himself flatter into the earth, trying to blend in, and snugged back his rifle, watching down its long barrel for movement up where their enemies were.

Behind Frank, Red Morton finally got Hogston to breathe again, and said: "Frank, you still figure I ought to leave you here alone?"

McCoy's answer sounded irritable. "Yes, I do. When me and Jackson Miggs got something interesting going we don't need any lowland cowboys to help us. Take that danged fool and get out of here. And tell Lex and Brian to keep out of this, too. Go on now, boy, beat it!"

Morton pushed Hogston into a crawling position, prodded him awkwardly as far as the first good stand of protective trees, then yanked Hogston upright and, using his six-gun, guided the captive eastward off through the forest.

Denver Holt called out in his rumblingly defiant voice, challenging Miggs to stand up, to fight man to man.

Miggs made no answer, but Frank did because he knew perfectly well that Jackson Miggs not only would not answer, but also that every second gained in parley with the Holts would help Miggs get that much closer.

"Sure!" yelled Frank. "You want it man to man, Holt, you show yourself first!"

This brought a string of vile epithets and McCoy grimly smiled before calling out again. "Holt, cussing isn't going to help you any. We've got Forrester and Hogston. So far none of us've been hurt. The odds are pretty big now . . . five to two of you, or maybe three, and we're on familiar ground. If you got the sense God gave a goose, you'll quit while you're still able."

Holt swore at Frank again, and, when McCoy laughed outright, one of the Holts fired down toward the sound of McCoy's voice.

The echo of that shot had scarcely died out when a fresh voice came down through the forest to McCoy. Miggs's voice. It was not particularly loud but its steely hardness gave it both depth and timbre.

"Get up you two. Easy, Bert . . . leave that gun on the ground."

Frank tensed unconsciously, tracked the location of that voice with his rifle barrel, and waited. It was not a long wait.

"Frank," called Jackson Miggs, "come on up here!"

Frank went without bothering to brush leaf mold and crumbly earth off his clothing. Once, he halted to whip around in response to the rush of oncoming booted feet. Fred Brian and Red Morton were recklessly dashing through the trees toward him. At first Frank's intention was to send those cowboys away. But on second thought he did not do this; instead, he led the cowmen on up where Miggs stood.

There were three men there. Four actually, but Jackson Miggs, who had craftily gotten completely around the others, was standing back a little distance with his cocked rifle covering the others.

One of those disheveled, unshaven, and ragged men who had survived the earlier stampede was moaning on the ground. This one had been shot along the ribs by Miggs's initial shot at the lot of them. The other two were Denver Holt and his son Bert. Neither of these two was hurt, but both were scratched, battered, and hatless. Most of the defiance was out of the younger man. His father, however, was as spittingly defiant as ever, unarmed or not. He glared at Frank and the two range men who had come up with Frank.

Miggs waited until Red, Frank, and Brian had halted, then said: "Spread out a little, boys. That's it. Now keep a sharp watch on 'em."

"What you fixing to do?" asked McCoy as Miggs lowered his rifle, leaned it gently against a tree, unbuckled his shell belt, and also hung this close by.

"We could shoot 'em, Frank," answered Jackson Miggs, "or hang 'em. They deserve one or both for coming up in here and acting like Comanches, stealing Beverly, pistol-whipping Brian, taking a shot at you . . . at all of us . . . and trying to ride roughshod over Tolman's range."

"Good idea," said Frank with a wolfish smile. "I'll go back and fetch a rope."

"But," went on Miggs, "I've got a better idea. Killing a man doesn't teach him anything."

Frank straightened back around, his brows drawing down. Brian and Red Morton looked puzzled, too.

Miggs thinly smiled at them, jerked his head to one side, and said: "Herd the old man away from the boy."

"*Ahhh,*" crooned McCoy, his face cleared instantly. "Of course. I didn't understand at first."

Brian and Morton still did not understand, but they aided McCoy in doing what Miggs had ordered, then, when Denver was glaringly apart from his son, Miggs moved down closer to the younger, taller man, deliberately went up close, slapped Bert Holt's face stingingly, and just as deliberately jumped back when Bert roared a curse and swung.

Denver Holt roared: "Get him, Bert! Beat him down and kick him to death, Son!"

Bert dropped his head, rushed in swinging, beat air, and whirled to come back again. Three times he did this and three times Miggs was not there when those punishing big fists whipped at roiled air where Miggs had been.

Bert, breathing hard, swore at Miggs. "Stand and fight, damn you. You wanted it like this . . . then stand and fight!"

Miggs did. He jumped out straight into the younger man's path exactly as he'd done with Curly Hogston before. Bert bored in at him. He struck Miggs three times, hard, and would have hit him again, but Miggs, hurt by those blows, lunged, whipped both arms around the larger man's waist, pinning his arms, locked his hands, and raised big Bert Holt half a foot off the ground at the same time burying his face against young Holt's chest.

Frank made a triumphant growl deep in his chest. When Denver Holt, seeing what Miggs was doing, would have jumped forward to succor his son, Frank's rifle barrel slammed across the big man's belly, stopping him cold, making Denver double over gasping. By the time Denver had his wind back and could straighten up, it was all over. Bert lay broken and twitching upon the ground, his face as red as sunset.

"Jack," asked Frank McCoy mildly, "you want this one now?"

Miggs nodded. He was sucking in great lungfuls of thin, high-country air, and staring across at old Denver Holt.

Fred Brian broke in. "Let me take the old man, Jackson. You're tired."

176

Miggs's face instantly and faintly clouded. He said nothing, only shook a peremptory arm at Morton and Fred Brian.

"Push him out here," he said to Frank. "Let's see just how tough he really is. If talk's any measure, then he'll eat me alive. Give him a shove, Frank."

McCoy roughly heaved Denver Holt forward.

The rugged old cowman minced ahead a little, side-stepping around Miggs and holding both massive, scarred fists low. He was not speaking now. In fact, he was not looking at all like the old arrogant, challenging Denver at all. He knew he was up against the fight of his life and meant to concentrate entirely upon this one thing.

Miggs turned as Holt circled him, but he gave no ground at all. He kept turning and Holt kept circling.

Finally Frank McCoy said sarcastically: "Jack, he's going to give you dancing lessons . . . he isn't going to fight."

That was when Denver Holt made his lunge. He came in low with one arm crooked up high to protect his face and chin, with his other arm straight out like a battering ram. It was a clumsy action, but, with all Holt's considerable weight behind it, if an opponent had been caught off guard, it could have dropped a man.

But Miggs, with thirty years of fighting behind him, was no greenhorn at rough-and-tumble. He'd guessed at once from the way Holt had circled around and around, what manner of battler the old cowman was, so, when Holt made his savage rush, Miggs dropped far down, threw all his weight in behind a cocked right fist, and fired it.

The blow whipped upward over Holt's bent arm, ground along Holt's forearm, ripping the sleeve, passed on through, and cracked with a loud report squarely between the cowman's eyes. Holt's own momentum had given Miggs's strike added impetus.

Holt's head snapped back. If his neck had not been as thick as the trunk of a young tree, it would have snapped under that violent, sledging blow. As it was Denver Holt threw up both arms, reeled back, stumbled over the legs of his unconscious son, and toppled. He struck the ground hard. Dust burst upward. He did not move again.

Fred Brian was the first to move, to make a sound. Fred bent to peer in amazement at those two big men lying there. "I'll be damned," he breathed.

The Holt range rider with his injured side forgot for this taut moment his own wound, to sit there dumbly staring.

All Jackson Miggs said was: "Red, go fetch the horses. It'll be suppertime before we get back."

Morton started, jerked back to the present by those quietly spoken words. "Sure," he said. "Yes . . . sir."

Frank walked over, leaned upon his rifle, and skeptically considered the Holts — father and son — spat aside, and kneeled to slap Denver Holt's face. It took a little time but when Red returned with Lex Murphy and the horses, Denver's eyes opened, rolled aimlessly for a moment, then gradually, wetly focused upon Jackson Miggs standing there with both arms hooked around his rifle.

Frank yanked Holt upright by his ragged shirt, pushed his thin, raffish face up close, and wickedly scowled. "You want some more?" he asked.

Holt didn't answer. His eyes had not entirely focused yet.

Frank roughly shook him by the shirt front and repeated the question.

This time Holt wagged his shaggy head from side to side, lifted his face, and gazed over at Jackson Miggs. "You win," he croaked huskily. "Mister Miggs, you win."

Jackson nodded. "All right, Mister Holt," he said. "Have your cattle out of the Ute Peak country by tomorrow afternoon."

"They'll be out, Mister Miggs. What about my riders?"

"We'll send 'em back to you, Mister Holt. And one other thing. That boy of yours . . . he's got some need for a strong hand on the reins. Someday he's going to touch the wrong girl again, and get himself killed."

Holt tried to rise up off the ground. If Frank and Red hadn't supported him, he'd never have made it, but, back upon his feet, he said: "You're right, Mister Miggs. He's near been the death of me before. You're plumb right. You've got my word for this . . . this time is the last time."

Miggs turned, went over to the horses, and swung up.

The others followed his example.

Frank McCoy squinted around. "Hey, Lex," he queried, "where's them cussed prisoners?"

"Tied to trees. Why?"

"Go set 'em loose," ordered McCoy, and turned his horse to head out.

They were halfway back toward Miggs's meadow when Fred Brian eased up beside Miggs, cleared his throat, looked a little apprehensive, and said: "Jackson . . . like I told you last night . . . there's something I'd admire to speak to you about."

Miggs looked quickly around, then away. That pained, worried expression mantled his rugged old features. He knew Frank McCoy had heard and was staring back at him, and this didn't help any.

"It's about Beverly."

Frank cleared his throat loudly and made an imperative frown at Miggs. "Well," said Frank, "answer him, consarn it."

Miggs did, but in a tone of diminishing force. "I know how it is with you, Fred. Sure, it's all right with me if it's all right with Beverly." Miggs looked relieved at having said this. Then he added: "But, Fred, when you bring up Tolman's cattle next summer . . ."

"Sure," said Brian gently, understanding a little of how the older man felt. "Sure, Jackson, I'll bring her with me."

"Now," pronounced Frank McCoy loudly, "maybe we can get a little dog-goned hunting done, Jack, since all this other stuff's taken care of."

180

About the Author

Lauran Paine who, under his own name and various pseudonyms has written over a thousand books, was born in Duluth, Minnesota. His family moved to California when he was at a young age and his apprenticeship as a Western writer came about through the years he spent in the livestock trade, rodeos, and even motion pictures where he served as an extra because of his expert horsemanship in several films starring movie cowboy Johnny Mack Brown. In the late 1930s, Paine trapped wild horses in northern Arizona and even, for a time, worked as a professional farrier. Paine came to know the Old West through the eyes of many who had been born in the previous century, and he learned that Western life had been very different from the way it was portrayed on the screen. "I knew men who had killed other men," he later recalled. "But they were the exceptions. Prior to and during the Depression, people were just too busy eking out an existence to indulge in Saturday-night brawls." He served in the U.S. Navy in the Second World War and began writing for Western pulp magazines following his discharge. It is interesting to note that all of his earliest novels (written under his own name and the pseudonym Mark Carrel) were published in the British market and he soon had as strong a following in that country as in the United States. Paine's Western fiction is characterized by strong plots, authenticity, an apparently effortless ability to construct situation and character, and a preference for building his stories upon a solid foundation of historical fact. *Adobe Empire* (1956), one of his best novels, is a fictionalized account of the last twenty years in the life of trader William Bent and, in an off-trail way, has a melancholy, bittersweet texture that is not easily forgotten. In later novels like *The White Bird* (1997) and *Cache Cañon* (1998), he showed that the special magic and power of his stories and characters had only matured along with his basic themes of changing times, changing attitudes, learning from experience, respecting Nature, and the yearning for a simpler, more moderate way of life.